Leo Kessler is a familiar name to readers of war fiction. In addition to his numerous super-selling war series he is the author of several non-fiction works and of the screenplay *Breakthrough*. He lives in Germany.

D1744792

Also by Leo Kessler

Leo Kessler

DEATH RIDE
Wotan 19

Futura

A Futura Book
First published in Great Britain in 1985 by
Centrury Publishing Co. Ltd.

First Futura edition 1985

Copyright © Charles Whiting 1985

All rights reserved
No part of this publication may be reproduced,
stored in a retrieval system, or transmitted, in any
form or by any means without the prior
permission in writing of the publisher, nor be
otherwise circulated in any form of binding or
cover other than that in which it is published and
without a similar condition including this
condition being imposed on the subsequent
purchaser.

ISBN 0 7088 2637 7

Printed in Great Britain by
Hunt Barnard Printing Ltd, Aylesbury, Bucks.

Futura Publications
A Division of
Macdonald & Co (Publishers) Ltd
Maxwell House
74 Worship Street, London EC2A 2EN

A BPCC plc Company

CONTENTS

'But here we are again like men redeemed from the grave
. . . We gave death the chance. Death did not take it and
we escaped alive.'

Siegfried Sassoon

PART ONE

Time Out Of War

'War is hell, but peacetime'll kill yer!'

Old Soldiers' Saying

CHAPTER 1

'PAREE–GAY PAREE!' Sergeant Schulze chortled hugely, as the truck bearing its cargo of dirty, lousy, ragged SS noncoms of SS Assault Regiment Wotan straight from the Russian front started to drive into a busy *Place Pigalle.*

'*Pig Alley itself!*' Schulze's running-mate Corporal Matz breathed. 'Pinch me! Am I dreaming?' He closed his eyes and swayed in the back of the crowded truck, as if he might faint at any moment. Hurriedly a couple of dozen felt-lice sprang from him to the tunic of the next man, like rats abandoning a sinking ship.

'Willya get a load of that hot steaming female gash, Matzi!' the big tough Hamburger said, bloodshot eyes gleaming excitedly as he took in the whores who were everywhere. 'Legs right up to their beautiful little female bums. Hold me, dear comrades, I think I'm just going to have my period. It's lust at first sight! *Hurrah!*' In a frenzy of excitement at the thought of what was soon to come, Sergeant Schulze took a mighty slug at his flatman, his adam's apple rushing up and down his neck like an express lift. With a wild whoop he threw the empty bottle of vodka over the side of the truck.

It exploded in a flurry of glass. The elegant French whores and their pimps in their flashy pin-striped suits and patent-leather shoes stared in awe at this collection of dirty, yelling, whistling SS men, as if they were creatures from another world – which, in a way, they were, though the French did not realise that.

The leave truck began to slow down. Hurriedly the NCOs grabbed for their packs, stuffed with the goods they would sell on the Parisian black market in order to pay for the whores.

Hastily Corporal Matz did the same, mind racing while he worked out how many whores he might get for a jar of real Popov caviare, but all the time not taking his greedy eyes off the tall, leggy whore who leaned against a lamppost, swinging her handbag carelessly, wet, crimson lips opened in delightful invitation. 'Look at that one, Schulze,' he breathed huskily, overcome with emotion at the sight of the big French whore in her rabbit-fur jacket and too-short skirt. 'She could blow my trombone any day! But the Great Whore of Buxtehude, where the dogs bark with their tails, you could get my bayonet into that lovely gob – *sideways* – easily!'

It was all too much for Sergeant Schulze. His face flushed a brick red with the bitter wind of the steppe, a lot of vodka, and excitement at the prospect of all 'the lovely grub' to come, he flung himself over the side of the still moving truck. He hit the cobbles of the *pavé* like a bag of wet cement. Schulze did not even notice. He lay writhing in the gutter in front of the crowd of awed whores, clutching his crotch as if he were in mortal agony, crying, 'Help me out of my agony, dear ladies of the night! Help me, I implore you, please! I haven't seen a piece of steaming female gash this side of 1941. If you don't help me instantly,' he moaned, looking up at the whores piteously (and, it must be admitted, directly up under their too-short skirts as well), 'I swear . . . *I'll just disintegrate. . .*' The big NCO's voice broke, as if with utter, overwhelming despair, as the truck braked to a halt and the eager noncoms began to drop to the ground. '*Here on this very spot, I shall simply explode into nothing!*'

But Sergeant Schulze was not destined to suffer that particularly nasty and untidy fate – just yet. For already Sergeant-Major Metzger, known behind his back as 'the Butcher'*, was taking up his stance in front of the impatient leave-men, ready to bring his own brand of sweetness and light into their sordid, brutal lives.

The huge Sergeant-Major, with his piglike eyes and shoulders like those of the oxen he had once slaughtered with one blow from his axe, took his time, savouring, as always, his power over Wotan's rank and file, telling himself that ever

---

* *Metzger* means 'butcher' in Southern German

since 1939 he had seen them come and go, swallowed up in the battles of the West and East, yet he, Sergeant-Major Alois Metzger, was still around, *surviving*.

Finally he assumed his favourite pose – the one he often practised in front of the mirror in the privacy of his own quarters: legs spread well apart, big paws on his hips, scarlet coward's face set in a look of absolute, overwhelming contempt and disgust, as if he could hardly bring himself to look at the horrors lined up in front of him. 'All right, you piss-pansies – and you two perverted banana-suckers, Schulze and Matz, get a load of this!' he bellowed.

Deliberately Schulze raised his right leg and gave one of his celebrated and not unmusical farts, dragging it out so that it had quite a pleasant effect. Indeed a couple of whores, who were not mesmerized by the sudden appearance of these huge, ragged men, were so impressed that they clapped in appreciation.

Gentleman of the old school that he was, Sergeant Schulze bowed in their direction modestly.

The Butcher was not so impressed. His bovine face flushed crimson. 'That's shitting dumb insolence that is, Schulze! Try that one more time and I'll sew up yer filthy arse so that yer'll have to fart out of yer ears! *Klar?*' he roared, scattering enraged spittle all over little Matz's face.

Schulze was not impressed. Nothing could spoil his sparkling mood this day. Matz, however, was. Deliberately he wiped the spit from his wizened face and said, 'Hey watch it, *Oberschar*! I had a bath three months ago, just before we invaded Popovland. I don't want to wash me skin away, yer know.'

Angrily the Butcher held up his middle finger, which looked like a hairy pork sausage. 'Sit on it, cunt!'

Matz, his good mood restored by the sight of the tall, leggy whore putting on more lipstick with great deliberation and much seductive rolling of her eyes, swallowed hard and said, 'No can do, Sergeant-Major. Already got a Berlin double-decker, yer see.'

The Butcher decided to ignore the Corporal. Besides, once he had delivered his little warning, he wanted to be on his way to that discreet little address recommended to him by one of his cronies, the kitchen bull, who apparently had the same problem as himself. 'Heaven, arse and cloudburst, Alois!' he had sworn dramatically, as he had handed the address over, 'the gash in that place could even give a mummy a hard-on!' Whereupon he had winked conspiratorially and had added *sotto voce*, 'They have their methods, you see! *Treatment*, they call it.'

'Right then, once again. This is the drill. You bunch of lucky shits have been given forty-eight hours here in Paris before you start training the new bunch of wet-tails being sent over from the Reich.' The Butcher puffed up his big chest for the benefit of the watching whores, telling himself that once he had received the mysterious 'treatment' they'd better watch their arses. A good piece of good German salami from Frau Metzger's handsome son would soon make their frog eyes sparkle – and then some. 'Now there's gonna be no trouble. You are representing SS Assault Regiment Wotan in this place and we want the frog-eaters to respect us, even if they do make love with their frigging mouths. *Ha ha!*'

Nobody laughed at his attempt at humour and Matz looked pointedly at his nails and said to Schulze, 'Could plant a nice crop of taties in that muck, Schulze, old comrade.'

The Butcher's face grew hard and his piglike eyes gleamed angrily. 'So this is the word. No milking mice. No piss-ups, no pox and no' – he wagged a finger at them warningly – 'frigging public scandals with the frog-eaters. Cos if there is, I tell yer this. The Vulture has promised to take a terrible revenge. Undoubtedly, he'll carve the frigging eggs off anybody who offends – *with a blunt razorblade!*'

Even Schulze shuddered at that terrible threat. Matz's little dirty paws flew to his crotch protectively and he whispered hoarsely to his running-mate, 'Christ on a crutch, Schulze, he wouldn't do that, would he? *Even* the Vulture wouldn't go that far!'

For the first time since they had entered Paris, Sergeant Schulze's tough young face showed doubt. For a moment he forgot the encouraging, impatient cries of the whores. He appeared even not to see the big fat one, who had lifted up her skirt and was crying happily in broken German, 'Here Fritz . . . look . . . best beaver in Paris!' pointing with her finger at her naked loins. 'Muff-time tonight, soldier boys!'

'I just don't know, Matzi . . . Warm brother that he is, that frigging Vulture has a heart of frigging stone.' And then he forgot their CO in far-off Metz. '*Los, Kameraden*,' he bellowed excitedly, breaking ranks and nearly knocking the Butcher over in his eagerness, 'let's point ourselves in the direction of the nearest knocking shop and begin to dance. For tonight, *Kameraden*, the glorious NCO Corps of SS Assault Regiment Wotan dances the mattress polka!'

'*Dance the mattress polka!*' a score of hoarse, eager young voices echoed the cry lustily, sending the pigeons roosting on the roofs of the 18th century buildings fluttering into the December sky in cawing protest.

SS Assault Regiment Wotan's time out of war had commenced . . .

But in spite of that terrible threat, Colonel Geier, known to his men as 'the Vulture', was not concerned with the antics of his surviving NCOs in Paris at that particular moment. Seated alone on a cold December afternoon in his gloomy quarters at the ancient caserne, some two hundred kilometres to the east in the Lorraine town of Metz, the hawk-nosed colonel concentrated his attention on those well-worn photographs which had accompanied him throughout the Russian campaign and which had been his only solace over the last terrible months when his regiment had been decimated by the Reds. Screwing his monocle more tightly into his right eye, feeling his pulse beginning to race with that old familiar excitement, he stared at the beautiful naked boys they portrayed, heart bursting with longing. Of course, he knew they were all *Strichjungen**, paid by professional pornographers to pose thus. But how young and beautiful they were! God in heaven, why couldn't he be in Berlin now, where boys like that were still available – at a price – if you knew where to look for them. Even that prude Himmler** could not stop them offering their delightful wares. The Vulture sighed again, self-pity overcoming him for a few moments so that a few sad tears rolled slowly down that rapacious face, dominated by its beak of a nose which had gained him his nickname.

Outside another batch of young recruits for Wotan were marching through the gates of the old French fort, singing that bold National Socialist marching song:

> 'Clear the street, the SS marches.
> The storm-columns stand at the ready;
> They will take the road
> From tyranny to freedom
> As did our fathers before us.
> Let death be our battle companion,
> We are the Black Band. . .'

The Vulture forgot his misery. The tears vanished as swiftly as they had come and his face twisted contemptuously. 'New cannon-fodder!' he sneered under his breath. In the same instant there was a polite knock on the door.

Hastily he slipped the pornographic photographs of the naked young men into the drawer, tugged at the Knight's Cross of the Iron Cross dangling from his skinny neck and barked, '*Herein!*'

Captain von Dodenburg, his left arm still in a sling, harshly handsome face pale from the weeks he had spent in the military hospital back in the Reich after being wounded in that disastrous retreat from Moscow, marched in and clicked smartly to attention. '*Obersturmbannführer*,' he snapped, 'new

*Slang for young male prostitutes
**Head of the SS

recruits for the First Company have just arrived. Will you speak to them, sir, or shall I dismiss them to their quarters immediately? They have been on the road with little food or drink for over thirty-six hours now, sir,' the handsome Captain with the bright-blue intelligent eyes added, his voice softer now.

Geier picked up his riding crop and set his peaked cap with that gleaming silver skull and crossbones insignia on his shaven head at a rakish angle. 'Von Dodenburg, you are too soft,' he sneered. 'The only way to achieve promotion in this army is to be as hard as Krupp steel. You *must* learn how to walk over dead bodies if you wish to succeed in Herr Hitler's vaunted Greater German Wehrmacht. Klar?' Regular officer that he had once been he could not refrain from sneering contemptuously at the name of the Führer.

'*Klar, Obersturmbannführer,*' von Dodenburg answered smartly, his pale face revealing none of the contempt he felt for the grotesque pervert who commanded SS Assault Regiment Wotan. He knew Geier had only transferred to the Armed SS in order to gain promotion more rapidly and achieve his overwhelming ambition – to become a general as his father had been before him. He felt nothing for the Holy Cause of the New Germany and those brave, noble boys from the Hitler Youth, eager to fight and die, if necessary, for their beloved Führer. But still, von Dodenburg told himself as he held the door open for the Vulture to pass through, the CO was probably the boldest and most capable commander of his rank in the whole of the SS. Even Jochen Peiper did not show the same kind of dash as the Vulture.

The Vulture took his time as he strode into the courtyard, watched by a couple of hundred eyes, as the new recruits stood rigidly to attention, flanked by the surviving two Mark III tanks, their steel flanks scored by Russian shells, which the Regiment had brought back from the disastrous retreat.

Slowly, very slowly, he straightened up to his full height in front of them, giving the draft a piercing look with his ice-cold

eyes, stroking his monstrous beak of a nose with one hand and
gently slapping his riding boot with the crop held in the other.
There was no sound except for the cawing of the rooks which
nested in the skeletal trees outside the barracks.

Suddenly the Vulture slapped his cane hard against his
boot. Even von Dodenburg started. 'Soldiers of the SS,' he
barked, 'my name is Geier. I have been told it's a name which
aptly suits my appearance.* 'He stroked his nose to emphasise
his point. No one smiled. Even these raw greenbeaks, a
watching von Dodenburg told himself, sensed just how
dangerous their new CO was. 'No matter. Now know this. At
present I am, as you can see, a humble colonel commanding a
regiment. But the war will be old before we can achieve that
final victory which our beloved Führer has promised us will
be ours.' He looked at von Dodenburg with a sneer on his face
and the latter felt himself flushing. The Vulture could never
resist a dig at Adolf Hitler. That he had escaped the clutches
of the Gestapo for so long was a plain miracle, von
Dodenburg could not help thinking. 'And by that time *Colonel*
Geier wishes to be *General* Geier, commanding a division just
as his worthy father did before him.' Geier pointed his cane
almost accusingly at the pale-faced, weary recruits. 'And how
will he achieve that highly laudable aim?' he barked, his
breath fogging the icy December air. 'I shall tell you. *On your
backs!*' He brought his cane down as if he were slashing some
poor recruit's naked back. 'You will make me my general's
stars. *By God you will if I have to kill the lot of you in the process!*'

His piercing gaze searched their rigid ranks, as if he were
looking for the least sign of weakness. But there was none. The
blond eighteen-year-old giants standing there in front of him
were the best that National Socialist Germany could produce
in this winter of 1941. All their young lives had been spent
preparing for this moment when they could wear the proud
black and white legend on their right sleeve: '*SS Assault
Regiment Wotan*'. For wasn't Geier's Wotan the premier

---

*Geier is the German for 'vulture'

regiment in the premier division of the whole of the *Waffen SS?*

The Vulture relaxed, obviously pleased with what he saw. 'Good, soldiers. I will not sing you an opera at this late hour. Your assignment is still secret. But I can tell you this. The next time SS Assault Regiment Wotan goes to the East, there will be no running away from the damned Ivans. *No sir!*' He slashed his cane against his gleaming boot to emphasize his point, one eye gleaming angrily through the silly monocle he affected in the style of the old-school regular officer.

Von Dodenburg frowned. Was that how the Vulture saw it? They had run away? Didn't he realise that the Regiment had been totally unprepared for the Russian winter? It was not the Ivans who had beaten them, but that damned 'General Frost', as they called their horrible winter weather.

'In my Regiment, we have a motto,' the Vulture was saying: 'train hard, fight soft. And that is what your task will be over the next weeks: *train . . . train . . . and train again!*' The Vulture paused and stared at their young faces, as if he were seeing them for the first time, trying to impress their features on his mind's eye for ever. 'But woe betide any one of you wet-tails who lets me down. I shall be merciless, absolutely ruthless. Make no mistake of that. Nothing, but nothing, must stand in the way of my becoming a general officer. *Do you understand that, soldiers?*' The Vulture's voice rose hysterically.

'*Jawohl, Obersturmbannführer!*' their hoarse young voices answered hastily, real fear in their eyes for the first time, as they realised that the honour of belonging to Wotan brought with it hidden dangers and threats they had never even dreamed of on the day they had volunteered for the SS in their naive youthful enthusiasm.

Von Dodenburg's heart went out to them. What must they think of an SS colonel who openly stated that his regiment had run away from those sub-humans, the Ivans, who admitted that his sole ambition was promotion? What indeed.

But now the Vulture was finished. He had seen his cannon-fodder and was satisfied they would serve his purpose for the few more months they would probably live. '*Gut, von Dodenburg,*' he announced almost wearily, 'get them out of my sight. Wheel them away.' Casually he touched his cane to the gleaming black visor of his cap and without another look at the draft turned and began to walk back to his quarters.

Von Dodenburg sighed and then dutifully 'wheeled them away'. It was all starting again. 'Train hard, fight soft,' the Vulture had proclaimed so boldly. But he had forgotten the third part of Wotan's motto, quoted behind the backs of the officers by the hard men of the NCO Corps, such as Schulze and Matz – '*and die soon . . .*'

CHAPTER 2

THE DESTRUCTION of SS Assault Regiment Wotan had commenced on that fateful Friday – Friday the thirteenth 1941. Just before dawn the troopers billeted in one of those nameless, God-forsaken villages to the west of Moscow had been awakened by a low, ominous rumbling to the east. Still half-asleep, heads heavy with the awesome amounts of vodka they had drunk the night before, the lice with which they were all infested by now as yet hardly stirring, they had dragged themselves grumpily from the ceiling-high tiled ovens on which they all slept for warmth and stumbled out of the straw-roofed *isbas** into a world which had been transformed, magically, overnight.

The day before everything had been mud, mud and yet more mud. Huge clumps of it had formed on their jackboots every time they walked anywhere. Non-tracked vehicles had sunk up to their axles in the thick, clinging black goo. Even tanks had thrown their tracks in the stinking muck.

Now all that had changed. An icy wind was racing savagely across the steppe straight from Siberia, cutting their shocked faces like a sharp blade, making them gasp with pain at every fresh breath. And everywhere there was a thick layer of brilliant white hoar-frost. Their tanks laagered in the village square were covered in what looked like heavy icing sugar. It was just like a scene from a cheap Christmas card. With one difference. To their front, the horizon was aflame, as if a dozen gigantic blast furnaces were shooting their flames into the dawn sky. And that was not all. Above the ever-rising rumble of the opening barrage, they could already hear the rusty squeak of tanks, hundreds of them – and they were

*Russian huts

all advancing on the positions held by SS Assault Regiment Wotan!

For what seemed an age, the shivering, unshaven, heavy-headed SS troopers simply stood there, mouths open and gaping like a collection of village yokels. For nearly five months now they had done nothing but advance, advance, advance, driving the defeated Ivans before them in panic until finally the November mud had bogged them down within sight of the enemy capital itself. Hadn't many of them collected abandoned Moscow tram tickets as souvenirs to show the folks back home when they goose-stepped in triumph and final victory through Berlin? *And now the Ivans were attacking . . ! attacking THEM!*

It was Sergeant Schulze who woke the mesmerised, sleep-drunk troopers to their danger. 'There's frigging Popovs over there at three o'clock!' he yelled in sudden alarm. 'Hundreds of the friggers . . . *LOOK!*'

Next to him Matz, trembling with cold, for he was standing in his underpants, a woman's fur tippet sent from the Reich around his skinny shoulders, whistled softly and said, 'Buy combs, lads . . . cos there's lousy times ahead!'

How right he was going to be, the little corporal at that moment could not have visualised in his wildest dreams.

The spell was broken. Everywhere whistles shrilled. Officers doubled back and forth. Red-faced, angry NCOs bellowed urgent orders. And all the time the barrage behind which the Russian infantry were now advancing came ever closer to the village and the Wotan positions.

The second shock came minutes later. '*Obersturm!*' the frantic cry went up on all sides, as the frustrated tank commanders discovered for the first time that it was not only the Ivans who were attacking them so surprisingly but 'General Frost' in person. 'We can't move the turrets . . . They're frozen solid, sir!'

Later von Dodenburg realised that he too had lost his head with the rest. Frantically he had hammered at the jammed turret with his fist, while his gunner, face glazed with sweat in spite of the icy wind, had exerted all his strength in an attempt to make the ten-ton turret move so that he could fire his 75mm cannon at the advancing Ivans. In vain! The damned thing had been frozen solid. The *Wehrmacht* had launched its surprise attack on Soviet Russia without the special greases and oils needed in that murderous climate to prevent moving parts from freezing up.

But the Vulture had kept his head amidst the confusion, the near-panic, the shells landing all around. 'Sergeant-Major Metzger,' he had bellowed above the ear-splitting racket as a Russian shell landed only metres away, showering him with frozen earth and pebbles, 'get headquarters company moving! Come on, you dogs, do you want to live for ever?' Beside himself with rage for having been caught off guard like this, he lashed out with his cane at the nearest soldier, fumbling with his helmet. '*Los . . . los . . .*'

Pale with shock and trembling visibly at the prospect of real shooting action after three years of total war, the Butcher somehow managed to get the cooks and clerks of the headquarters company together and before he had really understood what was happening he was charging forward with the Vulture, whooping his head off like 'a crazy chimneysweep', as he explained much later to his cronies, the kitchen bulls, straight towards the massed ranks of the Popovs.

Furiously von Dodenburg and his crew hammered at the locked turrets, using mallets, crowbars, even their naked fists, as the Russian infantry came ever closer and the clatter and rattle of tanks drowned even the roar of the creeping barrage.

In a few moments, von Dodenburg knew, his brain racing furiously, it would swamp their positions, then stop and allow the infantry to charge. Probably the Vulture and his scared collection of cooks and clerks might hold them for a minute or two, but what could even the Vulture do against a massed Popov attack? They had to free the turrets so that they could bring their guns to bear on the enemy T-34s. But how? *HOW?*

It was Schulze who came up with the solution. 'Gas!' he

yelled above the wild snap and crackle of the fire fight, as the Vulture engaged the Russian infantry. Tracer started zipping back and forth like flights of angry red hornets. 'Let's use our spare gas, sir!' Schulze ducked hastily as a salvo of slugs ran the length of the turret on his tank. '*Popov pricks!*' he cursed and waved a fist like a small steam-shovel at the solid line of advancing Russians.

'To do what?' von Dodenburg yelled back desperately.

'Douse the turrets in the juice, sir, and burn the buggers free. It's the only way!'

'Great crap on the Christmas tree, Schulze!' Matz breathed. 'You know the Vulture has promised five years of Torgau* to anybody wasting juice!'

'The Vulture can go and piss up his leg!' Schulze roared, already fumbling with the stiff, frozen cap of his tank's jerrican.

Von Dodenburg made his decision. Already the Vulture's little force was beginning to fall back before that solid wall of advancing infantry, from which rose that dread bass cry, '*urrah . . . urrah . . .*' As usual the Popovs had been well supplied with hundred per cent vodka before the attack; they would go to their deaths like lemmings, dead drunk but happy. 'Burn the buggers loose, as Sergeant Schulze says!' he bellowed as the barrage came ever closer, throwing up huge mushrooms of frozen earth into the grey lowering sky. 'At the double now . . . *dalli dalli* . . .!'

The tankers needed no urging. They all knew the next few minutes would decide whether they lived or died. With frantic, fumbling fingers that felt like clumsy sausages, they fought to open the frozen cans. Abruptly the air was flooded with the stink of gasoline. Hastily the tankers thrust home the ends of their rolls of toilet paper, soaking them with gas. 'Don't go to the thunderbox this morning and wipe yer ass,' Schulze chortled crazily, 'not with this crap paper . . . or you'll be in for a good big surprise, comrades!' Laughing

*Notorious German military prison

wildly he dropped from the tank and lit a match. It spurted alight. Schulze touched it to the end of the roll. It began to blaze immediately. He wasted no more time. With a grunt he heaved the burning roll of toilet paper at the gas-soaked turret and jumped back.

Just in time. With a great *whoosh*, the gas exploded. In an instant the turrets of the Mark IIIs were blazing merrily everywhere, their paint bubbling and scarring like the symptoms of some loathsome skin disease.

Now as the Russians' shells exploded all around them, the tankers crouched impatiently waiting for the flames to die out, casting glances to their front anxiously, knowing that if they didn't go into action soon, they would be overrun by the enemy, for already the survivors of the Vulture's bold attempt to hold up the Russians were streaming back in panic. Furiously the Vulture, his face crimson with rage, lashed out at them with his cane, in between snapping off shots from his pistol at the packed ranks of the Russians. But there was no holding the terror-stricken cooks and clerks. Here and there some of them even dared to throw away their weapons and flee blindly to the rear, never to be seen again: an event which allowed the Butcher to find a way out of his own problem, the fact that he was 'scared shitless' as Schulze put it contemptuously later. 'Let me form a skirmish line – to the rear, sir!' he bellowed above the racket, eyes wide with unreasoning fear. 'I'll stop the rot, *Obersturmbannführer!* The rotten shitheels won't escape me!' Even before a breathless Colonel Geier could answer, he was off at a run, disappearing into the fog of war for the rest of this day's combat.

But the tankers had no time for the panic and fear of Sergeant-Major Metzger. Now the blue flames were beginning to die out and already to their front the Russian officers were drawing their sabres. Silver flashed. A great bass roar came up from the massed ranks. Red flags were waved, bugles blown. '*SLAVA KRASNAYA ARMYA!*' they cried, their war-cry echoing back and forth between the hills.

'Here they come!' von Dodenburg yelled desperately. He

doubled forward. Yelping with pain as he touched the red-hot metal of the turret, he swung himself inside.

The gunner followed an instant later. Below, the driver scrambled into his seat. Furiously von Dodenburg and the gunner cranked the turret, as the driver pressed his starter button. The Russians were only one hundred and fifty metres away now, stamping forward in a ragged run, long bayonets gleaming in the first slanting rays of the blood-red sun. Time was running out . . . fast. Suddenly it moved. The turret started to turn! Below the Mark III's 400HP engine burst into noisy, throaty life. All along the line other engines did the same.

Von Dodenburg pressed his throat-mike urgently. 'Tiger to all,' he cried, 'Tiger to all . . . *ADVANCE!*' With his right foot he kicked the driver's shoulder. It was the signal to move out. Hurriedly he thrust home the first of his twenty-odd gears. The tank lurched forward. Von Dodenburg grabbed hold of the nearest stanchion hurriedly and winced with pain as he looked to left and right. Like monstrous metal ducks, his tanks had begun moving forward, the gunners swinging their turrets to left and right to ensure they would work correctly when they met the Russian tanks . . .

'Going through 'em like shit through a goose!' Schulze yelled exuberantly over the radio, as his tank battled its way through the screaming, panic-stricken mass of Russian infantry, flailing those in its path to bloody pulp, churning up their limbs so that they lay in the wake of the Mark III pressed into the frozen earth like men made of cardboard. With him in the turret, Matz, carried away by the wild, cruel blood-lust of battle, swung the machine-gun from left to right, whooping like a crazy Red Indian as he mowed the running Russian infantry down. It wasn't war; it was plain, brutal murder. The Russian infantry simply did not have a chance against the thirty-ton monsters.

But leading the great V of metal now spread out across the frozen steppe, von Dodenburg told himself that they had just achieved an easy victory. Soon they would bump into the

enemy's armour and then things would be different. He knew
his Mark IIIs were no match for the new Russian T-34s. The
only way he could beat them would be by surprise and
cunning.

'*Popov* T-34s . . ! *One . . . two . . . six of them, sir!*' his gunner
yelled suddenly, the fear in his voice all too obvious.

'Where?'

'Three o'clock, sir,' the gunner answered, already crouching
behind the sight of his stubby 75mm cannon. 'Next to that
patch of firs, sir.'

Von Dodenburg gasped with shock. They were the new T-
34s all right and the whole bunch of them were already
bellied down so that only their turrets and great long
overhanging 75mm cannon were visible. '*Shit, shit, shit!*' he
cursed. Every advantage seemed to be on the Popovs' side.
His brain raced furiously. What was he going to do? *What?*

To his front, scarlet flame stabbed the smoke with startling
suddenness. A solid white armour-piercing shell raced
towards him, gathering speed with every second. '*Right . . !
brake right, driver!*' Von Dodenburg screamed hysterically.

The driver reacted instinctively. The tank reeled to one
side, throwing up a huge shower of dirt and pebbles. The
killer shell howled by them. Next moment it slammed into the
side of the Mark III behind von Dodenburg's. There was the
great hollow boom of metal striking metal. The Mark III
came to an abrupt, awkward halt, as if it had suddenly run
into a brick wall. For what seemed a long time nothing
happened. Then suddenly a great searing flame ran the
length of its deck like a mighty blowtorch. White-glowing
pieces of steel erupted into the air. Screaming, frantic tankers,
uniforms already well ablaze, dropped to the ground,
staggered a few paces and then fell, writhing piteously back
and forth, their struggles growing weaker by the second until
finally they could move no more and lay still, letting the
greedy blue flames have their way.

Von Dodenburg turned away sickened. It would be only a
matter of minutes before his whole command became a

collection of similar burning wrecks if he didn't act soon and decisively. He pressed his throat-mike with a hand that trembled badly. 'Tiger to all,' he commanded hastily, hardly recognising his own voice, 'fire white smoke . . . Blind the Popov pricks . . . and then –'

His words were drowned by the banshee-like shriek of another Russian AP shell. It flashed across his front in an electric-white blur. A Mark III breasting a small rise had exposed its under-protected soft belly and the Russian gunner had not waited for a second invitation. The Mark III didn't have a chance. It flew apart in one tremendous, ear-splitting roar. Even at a distance of two hundred metres, von Dodenburg standing in the open turret could feel the blast slap him cruelly across the face, snatching the very air out of his lungs, as the tank disappeared in a burst of grey-yellow smoke. When it cleared, all that was left was a severed head rolling lazily across the steppe like a football abandoned by some careless child.

Now the Wotan gunners took up the challenge. Everywhere white phosphorus shells began to explode to the front of the hurrying tanks. Thick white smoke started to stream upwards almost immediately. Within seconds a smoke screen, blinding the Russian gunners, began to form. Urgently von Dodenburg pressed his throat-mike once more. 'Hit the tube, you drivers!' he bellowed above the racket. '*Ran wie Bluecher!*'*

His drivers needed no urging. They knew that as long as the smoke held they were relatively safe. But by the time it cleared, they had to be in among the superior Russian tanks, battling it out, or they would be destroyed. They roared forward, throwing up huge showers of flying gravel and earth before them.

In the middle of that lethal steel V plunging through the choking white smoke, von Dodenburg, bolt-upright in his turret, tensed, waiting for the first sight of the enemy. A hundred metres to his right Schulze did the same, keeping his

---

*At them like Bluecher (the famous Prussian commander)

CO covered. Normally Schulze had no time for 'officers and shitting gents', as he called them contemptuously. But von Dodenburg was different. He did not throw away his men's lives just in order to 'cure his throatache'* and decorate his manly breast with 'tin'.** Von Dodenburg looked after his soldiers and Mrs Schulze's handsome son was not prepared to have him shot by some 'Popov prick' unnecessarily.

'Right you bunch of reluctant heroes,' von Dodenburg's voice came crackling over the ether excitedly, 'there they are . . . between two and three o'clock . . . Select your targets . . . I think we've caught them with their drawers down. *FIRE AT WILL!*'

'Holy strawsack!' Schulze cursed and slapped Matz heartily on the back. 'Stick a piece of steel salami up the arse of that one to the right, Matzi!'

Matz needed no urging. He peered through the sight, its calibrated glass neatly dissecting the rear – the weakest point – of a still unsuspecting T-34 facing in the wrong direction. He flashed a glance at the fire control. The red light burned steadily. His little hand sought and found the firing lever. He forced himself to breathe more evenly. He'd only get one chance. Slowly, very slowly, he eased the lever back.

Suddenly the 75mm cannon erupted into violent, furious activity. There was a tremendous crack. The green-glowing turret filled with acrid smoke. The breech came sliding back. A gleaming yellow cartridge case, exuding white smoke, clattered to the metal deck as the white blur of the AP shell sped relentlessly towards the still unsuspecting Russian.

It struck the T-34 with a terrific impact. The Russian tank shook violently, white smoke erupting almost immediately from its shattered engine. Its right track slithered to the ground like a broken limb. At once its crew started to clamber out, hands already raised in surrender. But there was going to be no quarter given this day. Somewhere a machine-gun chattered like an irate woodpecker. The Russians went

*i.e. gain the Knight's Cross, worn around the neck
**Decorations

reeling from side to side, what looked like red buttons stitched across the chests of their brown coveralls.

Now everywhere the Mark IIIs came trundling out of the thick smoke, cannons blazing, bringing the battle to the Russians even before the latter had realised that they had been tricked. Within the first five minutes ten T-34s lay wrecked on the steppe, blazing furiously, as the tankers of SS Assault Regiment Wotan slammed into their positions with unstoppable élan and energy.

But even in this moment of local victory, von Dodenburg knew, with a sinking heart, that the German Army had gained only a temporary respite. Even as his gunner knocked out another T-34, von Dodenburg's earphones were filled with frantic, panic-stricken pleas for help in German. Everywhere the *Wehrmacht's* front before Moscow was breaking down under a merciless full-scale Russian attack – rapidly. Even as he ordered the bold tank-thrust to be broken off, von Dodenburg told himself miserably that the time to run for their very lives had commenced . . .

How he lived through that terrible next week before he was finally wounded and evacuated, von Dodenburg never really knew. In retrospect it seemed to have been a confused, panicked mixture of stand, fight, run, stand, fight, run. Over and over again, all day and all night. And each time the ragged, utterly weary Wotan would leave behind it on that limitless plain yet another score or so of bold young men who would never see their homeland again, their stiffened, mutilated bodies rapidly disappearing for good beneath that relentless white curtain of snow.

On the third day of that headlong retreat westwards, their wake strewn with abandoned equipment, vehicles that had run out of fuel, bloodstained faeces – for they all had what they called the 'thin shits' now – and bodies, Siberian ski troops cut them off from the rest of the division. The Vulture was not overly worried. Confidently he told what was left of his young officers, their faces purple with the awesome cold, eyelashes white with hoar-frost, 'Corps will carve us out, gentlemen. Never fear. SS Assault Regiment Wotan is far too precious to those gentlemen up top for them to let it be wasted in this God-forsaken arse of the world!'

But the Vulture had been wrong. Corps itself was in full retreat now and on the fourth day all radio contact with it was lost. Now the air waves were full of the crash and blast of Soviet military music which jammed any attempt to contact other German units. As Schulze commented to Matz, wrapped in what appeared to be a horse blanket – at least it smelled like that – an opaque dewdrop suspended from the end of his pinched, pink nose: 'Matzi, now the clock is well and truly in the piss-pot!'

It was! On the fifth day, after they had been forced almost to a standstill by the streaming, merciless snow-storm and repeated attacks by the white-clad Siberians who came hissing in on their skis with reckless courage, the Vulture finally conceded the seriousness of their situation. Sheltering behind one of the surviving Mark IIIs, its engine still running in spite of the shortage of fuel – otherwise it would have frozen up immediately – he said, 'Gentlemen, comrades, as that celebrated French commander said at Sedan* back in 1870, "We have been caught in a piss-pot – and now the enemy is going to shit upon us!"'

His attempt at bitter humour failed lamentably. His officers were simply too weary. Numbly, most of them shivering with the cold like young puppies, they waited for his decision in silence.

It came with the Vulture's old brutal harshness. 'I am going to load every fit man onto the remaining Mark IIIs and make a breakout,' he snapped, his breath fogging the air in little grey clouds. 'All unnecessary equipment will be destroyed. We must travel light if we are going to succeed. Questions?'

No one dared, save von Dodenburg. 'Yes,' he said, his voice

---

*A siege-battle during the Franco-Prussian War of that year

cracked and husky with fatigue, 'what about the wounded, *Obersturm?*'

'They will be left behind. Anyone who cannot hold a weapon, von Dodenburg, is simply a useless luxury.' The Vulture forced a cold, wintry smile. 'Is that not the philosophy of you gentlemen of the SS? Ruthlessness, even against one's self, is absolutely necessary if one is to succeed. *Gemeinnutz geht vor Eigennutz, was?*'*

Von Dodenburg nodded his head in defeat. 'I will take care of . . . the wounded personally, *Obersturm*,' he whispered, his voice choked and broken.

'Do that, von Dodenburg,' the Vulture said lightly, as if it were every day that he allowed one of his officers to shoot twenty or so of their own wounded. 'And tell them all before you do it what brave fellows they were – *are*. Their sacrifice for our beloved homeland will never be forgotten, even after a thousand years. Now, *meine Herren*, I shall take the point – here . . .'

Some of them had pleaded with the young officer, his pistol already in his hand. They had cried for their mothers, for God, for their Führer: anyone who would show them mercy and save them from their fate, their poor young faces contorted with pain and fear. Others had accepted what was soon going to happen to them stoically, asked for a last cigarette, taken a few puffs and turned their heads, eyes closed, waiting for that final shot which would rip away the back of their skulls and propel them into oblivion. A few had been fervent, fanatical National Socialists to the very end, bravely crying out '*Sieg Heil*' while trying to give the 'German Greeting'** at the very moment that a weeping von Dodenburg placed the muzzle of his pistol against the base of their skulls and pressed the trigger.

In the end it had been done and he had stood there, staring at their shattered faces, his shoulders heaving like a

---

*A popular Nazi motto: 'the good of the community is more important than that of the individual.'

**i.e. the Nazi salute

heartbroken child, pistol dangling from nerveless fingers. Silently, Schulze had guided him through the great wet flakes of falling snow back to his tank. One hour later the armour-piercing shell had slammed into the side of the turret, a terrible burning pain blazed the length of his right arm, and he had slumped almost immediately into blessed unconsciousness.

Lying on his bunk, listening to the night sounds made by the new draft . . . the rattle of mess-tins, the crunch of their heavy boots on the gravel as they struggled with their new mattresses, the odd youthful laugh – von Dodenburg thought of those dead young men lying back there in the snow, a couple of thousand kilometres from where he was now. He could still see their dead eyes staring up at him accusingly afterwards as Sergeant Schulze had led him away. Those eyes burning into him would haunt him all his days until he too was swallowed up into the greedy maws of the God of War. Now he was expected to do it again: to teach those young boys out there to fight – and to die. Could he do it yet once more? Had he the courage, the spirit, the coldness of heart to do that, when he knew, in the end, they would have to sacrifice their young lives like all those who had gone before them?

He didn't know. Hugging his aching arm, which had still not healed properly, he drifted into an uneasy sleep, lying there stretched out on his bunk perfectly straight, hardly seeming to breathe. To any casual observer, Kuno von Dodenburg might well have been already dead . . .

CHAPTER 3

CORPORAL MATZ squatted morosely in the back of the leave-truck, a pair of red satin frilly knickers wrapped around his shaven skull for warmth, sipping beer from a highly ornate chamber pot that he had stolen from the last whore he had danced 'the mattress polka' with. Next to him a burly sergeant sawed wood loudly, while another of the exhausted leavemen kept repeating doggedly, 'But I only asked her if she'd ever done it with a feather, comrades. She had no reason to throw the fucking bed at me, did she now . . .?'

Matz ignored both of them. He concentrated on the beer, although it was only just dawn. Outside in the street, surly frog civilians cycling to work in the war factories, cigarettes glued to their bottom lips, studiously ignored the drunken, snoring SS men.

He was broke, had a stinking headache and now harboured a sneaking suspicion that the last but one whore he had pleasured – the one with the two sets of tits – might well have given him a little *souvenir de Paris* to take home to Metz with him. At least he half-suspected that from the way he had been pissing in six different directions since yesterday evening. He took another swig of the French beer and said mournfully, 'And you with the frigging hammer at the back of my turnip, will yer stop swinging it!' But the persistent throbbing at the top of his poor head continued. He closed his eyes.

But not for long.

'*I drink to forget . . . I drink to forget . . . But I've forgotten what it was . . . I drink to forget . . .*' That drunken, well-remembered voice penetrated insidiously into his black reverie. Moodily Matz opened his eyes, closed them again rapidly, then opened them once more, a sudden look of total disbelief on his wizened face.

It was Schulze, of course. Who else could it be? But he had

been somehow transformed he realised as the French pedal-taxi man, panting and red-faced under the big NCO's weight, rolled gratefully to a stop. Now both Schulze's eyes were blackened and almost closed and his nose had swollen to the size of a miniature football.

Matz sat up as Schulze stumbled out of the pedal-taxi, grandly handing the exhausted cyclist a wad of useless French currency. 'Here my man, take this arse-paper and remember to light a frigging candle for my soul when you next go to the frigging synagogue!' Laughing hugely at his own feeble humour, he took a final swig at the bottle of champagne he was cradling in his arms and tossed it into the gutter.

Matz shook his head in wonder, even though it hurt like hell, and called, 'Where in three devils' name did you get those violets from?' He indicated Schulze's black eyes. 'And that beautiful red hooter?'

Schulze grinned drunkenly. 'What the prick was called I don't know, you little asparagus Tarzan,' he announced, obviously very pleased with himself. 'But I'd know him again if I ever met him.'

'Why?' Matz asked stupidly.

'*Cos I've got his left ear in me frigging pocket!*' Schulze cried and slapped the side of his tunic as he stumbled towards the truck, one hand held out in front of him like a blind man feeling his way. Matz heaved. With a sigh of relief, Schulze collapsed on the floor next to the burly sergeant who was still sawing wood, just as Sergeant-Major Metzger came limping round the corner, a look which boded no good on his brick-red butcher's face.

'Are you all there?' he barked, supporting himself by a cane which he had acquired somewhere or other, something which looked suspiciously like the broken chain of a pair of handcuffs dangling down the side of his left sleeve. 'Cos, I'm not frigging well waiting for nobody . . . Can't frigging well get back to Metz soon enough!' he added, almost as if he were talking to himself.

In his sleep Sergeant Schulze blew the strangely distraught Butcher a wet, dreamy kiss and said in a far-away voice, 'Will you tuck me into my little bed later, Sergeant-Major?'

Curiously enough even Schulze could not rile the Butcher this day. Instead of flying into a rage he clambered very stiffly into the back of the truck, even though the seat of honour next to the driver in the cab was naturally reserved for his august person, and stood hanging on to a stanchion in the freezing wind for the whole of the long journey back to Metz. As Schulze commented later to his running-mate Matz, 'Yer know Matzi, if I didn't know that our senior sergeant was a big feller now, I'd have bet my last week's pay, which I don't have no more, that he's had his big fat fart-cannon tanned like some shitty-arsed little kid, that I would . . .'

And strangely enough that was exactly what *had* happened to Sergeant-Major Alois Metzger during his soujourn in *La belle Paris* in search of the 'treatment' which had been so highly recommended to him by his crony, the kitchen bull. But unfortunately in his case it had not had the same effect that it had had on that celebrated Egyptian mummy. Not only had his libido taken a terrible beating in the last forty-eight hours in Paris, but several other parts of his person as well . . .

'So you are back at last, you filthy swine!' the Vulture had welcomed them gratingly, as they had dropped stiffly from the leave-truck, stamping their feet to try to bring some life back to those solid blocks of ice. He had screwed up his eye around the silly monocle he affected and had stared at them as if they were some particularly unpleasant form of life. 'You have had your disgusting piggeries no doubt, sticking your filthy . . . er . . . things in those poxed whores, drinking that rotgut, and obviously from the looks of you' – he had peered hard at Schulze's battered face – 'causing scandals about which I will undoubtedly hear in due course from the commanding general. Well, the good times are over, *meine*

Herren. All of you will proceed *immediately* to the MI Room*
where you will all have your disgusting sexual organs well
irrigated before it is too late and will report for duty *at once*
thereafter!'

'Sir . . .' The Butcher had raised his hand, trying to avoid
the customary post-coital treatment which entailed sticking
up a rubber tube and irrigating the 'filthy thing', as the
Vulture called it, with burningly hot potassium permanganate.
'I don't think I need it, sir,' he said in a wary voice.

'*Don't need it!* Why, Sergeant-Major Metzger, haven't you
indulged yourself with those filthy French whores, eh?'

Schulze nudged Matz. 'Didn't I allus tell yer the Butcher
was off? Betcha it's fallen off from too much five against one
when he was young.' He made an obscene rubbing gesture
and chuckled softly.

'Well, no, not exactly, sir,' the Butcher replied, face
turning crimson with embarrassment, head turned to one
side as if he were finding it very difficult to express himself.
'It's sort of difficult to explain, sir –'

It was just then that the Vulture caught sight of the strange
chain dangling from the big NCO's wrist and snapped, 'And
what in three devils' name is that on your wrist, Metzger?'

The Butcher blushed an even deeper red and stuttered,
'It's sort of a chain . . . er . . . *a charm bracelet*, sir.' He let his
gaze fall to the ground under the Vulture's hard scrutiny.
'Yessir, a charm bracelet,' he repeated.

Schulze whistled softly beneath his raised hand and
exclaimed, 'So that's it! It ain't bad enough that we've got a
CO who likes little boys' arses. Now we've a sergeant-major
who's a warm brother.** Christ on a crutch, what's the
frigging Wotan coming to?'

In the end the Vulture dismissed them – all save the
Butcher whose 'charm bracelet' seemed to have done the
trick – to the MI Room for the treatment. There the
exhausted, hollow-eyed NCOs lined up in front of the long

*Medical Inspection
**Homosexual

zinc counter and irrigated their sexual organs with the long
rubber tubes filled with the burning solution like so many
horses being watered at the end of a long day, while outside
the draft commenced their training. 'Here we go again,
Matzi,' Schulze sighed wearily, supporting himself with his
left hand while he held his penis lovingly with the other, 'into
the tatties, out of the tatties.' He shook his head. 'I wonder
what the Greatest Captain of All Times* has got in frigging
store for us at the end of this little lot? I just wonder.' He shook
his big head like a man sorely tried and then concentrated on
squirting the purple liquid up his precious penis . . .

It was a problem that occupied Captain von Dodenburg too,
as Christmas 1941 approached and the training of the new
recruits reached its peak. It was obvious that eventually the
Regiment would return to Russia; all the new equipment
arriving daily at the caserne – white camouflaged coveralls,
thick padded jackets of a completely new design, special
Arctic greases and oils for their weapons, felt overshoes –
clearly indicated that. But as yet they had not received any
new Mark IIIs to replace those lost in the disastrous retreat
from Moscow, while daily, when he went into the centre of
Metz for treatment for his arm, he could see the marshalling
yards full of Mark IIIs being sent to other armoured
regiments stationed in the area. It was quite a mystery.

But von Dodenburg had other problems on his mind that
freezing third week of December on his trips to the military
hospital, which lay not far from Metz Cathedral. Now the
Vulture had ordered live ammunition to be used during
training, although von Dodenburg had protested the new
boys were not ready for it. 'Get the wet-tails used to shot and
shell, von Dodenburg!' the Vulture had overridden his
protest brutally. 'They'll be dead soon enough as it is anyway.
Your young heroes will only be too happy to die for me – *and*

---

*The soldiers' cynical nickname for Adolf Hitler

their beloved Führer too, naturally,' he had added with a cynical, twisted smile on his thin, cruel lips. 'Live ammo it is, von Dodenburg.' So it was that when he was driven to the hospital for his daily treatment, more often than not he was accompanied by some moaning, ashen-faced youth, who had been shot during training by one of his own NCOs.

It was in that same third week of December with the 'grey mice', as the burly but homely German nurses were called behind their backs by the patients, already beginning to decorate the wards for Christmas, that he met Doctor Claudine Louis for the first time. *Oberarzt* Lochner himself introduced the young SS officer to the French doctor with a grin on his ancient face. 'Here you are, young von Dodenburg, I've decided you need a change of doctor, someone with a prettier mug than mine. Might accelerate your cure, what? Doctor Louis . . . Captain von Dodenburg.'

Her hand had been as cool and as firm as her face, beautiful in that olive-brown, long-nosed fashion of the Southern French, her dark eyes revealing nothing as *Oberarzt* Lochner left them and she began to examine the taut pink skin which had now begun to cover the hole left by the Russian shell fragment. 'Move your shoulder please,' she commanded in her excellent German. Later he would discover she had studied for a time at Heidelberg before the war. 'Let us see how your muscles function.'

She had bent over him to feel his shoulder and he could smell her fragrance and feel the warmth of a hot-blooded, passionate woman beneath that cool exterior. 'Well,' he asked, eyes full of interest, 'what is *Madame Le Docteur*'s opinion?'

'*Mamselle*,' she corrected him routinely, her own face revealing nothing. 'Another two weeks or so and you'll have one hundred per cent articulation once more. I am sure' – she took her hand from his naked shoulder and indicated that he could slip into his bemedalled tunic again – 'you will be certified fit for combat once more. There are surely a few more bits of er tin, as I believe you call it, that you can win, *hein?*'

She looked at him directly, as he paused in his dressing. But again that smooth olive face revealed nothing. Was she making fun of him with her reference to 'tin'? For the first time in years von Dodenburg, hard-bitten veteran of combat on two continents, found himself actually blushing . . .

Now with Christmas Eve, the greatest German festival of the year, only twenty-four hours away, the training of the reformed SS Assault Regiment Wotan went on relentlessly. The Vulture would tolerate no letting-up, no relaxing of the pressure, even though the first snows of the winter had now begun to fall over Lorraine and in the mornings the water in the troughs in which the recruits – stripped naked – washed was frozen solid. 'It's march or croak, von Dodenburg!' he snapped, slapping his cane against his highly polished boots, watching with interest as the naked youths scampered through the snow to wash in the troughs, the steam rising from their hardy, muscular bodies like that from a bunch of overheated plough horses. 'They are fine young specimens, the best your Hitler Youth can produce . . .' Von Dodenburg ignored the 'your' and waited. '. . . They can stand the strain and pace. It's the assault course for them this morning, von Dodenburg.' The Vulture swallowed hard, straining hard to keep his voice from breaking. What beautiful bodies they did have! *Himmelherrgott*, it was more than a man could stand, seeing them running around naked like that!

Von Dodenburg saluted and the Vulture strode away as if he were in a great hurry to get back to the warmth of the regimental office, which the younger officer would well appreciate. Only a fool – '*and an SS man*', the cynical little voice at the back of his mind whispered maliciously – would attempt Wotan's assault course on a freezingly cold morning before Christmas like this one.

They commenced immediately after their spartan breakfast of acorn coffee and milk soup, each man laden down with thirty kilos of equipment, steel helmet and rifle. The first time it was bad: a narrow plank covered with ice and suspended over a ten-metre drop; a hundred-metre crawl under knee-high barbed wire with the instructors firing bursts of live ammunition just above their helmeted heads; a terrifying lunge for a slip rope an arm's length away to swing over a torrent of wild, white water, the grinning instructors tossing grenades into it all the time, sending up huge spouts that threatened to tear them from the rope at any minute; a final five rounds rapid fire with the targets swaying and trembling like crazy things in front of their eyes which bolted out of their scarlet faces like those of madmen.

That was the first time.

'Not good enough!' the Vulture barked, eyes on his stop-watch. 'Lot of soft wet-tails. Three minutes too slow. Sergeant-Major Metzger, wheel them through it again!'

'*Jawohl, Obersturmbannführer,*' the butcher bellowed happily. As always, he enjoyed it when others suffered, even now after his own unfortunate experiences in Paris. 'All right, you bunch of arses with ears, you heard the Colonel. *Los!*'

So they did it a second time. Their knees were like rubber, their chests heaved like cracked bellows, their faces were glazed with sweat in spite of the biting cold. Even some of the young giants who had been hardened by years of para-military training in the Hitler Youth began to break down, sobbing openly as they staggered from one obstacle to the next as if they were drunk.

Still the Vulture was not satisfied. 'One minute too much!' he declared, while von Dodenburg fumed at his side, his fists clenched to prevent himself from physically attacking the Vulture.

The Butcher smiled happily. Perhaps this night, with a few good shots of schnaps under his belt, he would try one of the mess waitresses. The frog gash would know better than to disobey him when he ordered them to whip them down – he winced mentally at his choice of words. Immediately it brought back terrible memories of what had happened in Paris. Still, tonight he'd try again. It might just work. After all, Christmas was coming up and he did deserve a little present of some sort. 'All right, you piss-pansies! let's do it again –'

He stopped short suddenly. There was a tremendous noise coming from the cobbled street outside. It sounded like a whole squadron of heavy Junkers bombers in full flight, accompanied by the squeak and rattle of what could only be tank tracks.

Even the Vulture forgot the assault course now, as the great roar grew louder and louder, echoing back and forth down the streets outside. He turned and stared at the gate of the *Sepp Dietrich Kaserne**, as the old French caserne was now renamed.

There, the helmeted sentries were hurriedly raising the red and white striped barrier, the awe in their young faces all too evident, and then springing back out of the way as if they were suddenly scared for their lives.

Schulze, standing just behind the Vulture, stared at Matz enquiringly.

His running-mate shrugged eloquently. Who am I – Jesus? No, I don't frigging well know what it is!'

Schulze was too intrigued by the source of that tremendous noise even to attempt to find a suitable reply; besides, Matz would never have heard him now. The racket was ear-splitting. The very walls of the caserne shivered and trembled like a live thing. Here and there plaster started to rain down in a grey storm. The windows creaked and groaned, as if they might crack at any moment.

Suddenly there was the tremendous noise of gears being slammed home. The engine of whatever it was whined into low gear. A cloud of dust rose in a quick mushroom beyond the wall of the caserne. Hastily a group of French cyclists on their way to work braked to a stop opposite the gate and pressed themselves against the nearest wall, eyes full of fear. And then suddenly, dramatically, frighteningly, there it was.

*The name of the first commander of the Armed SS

A massive wall of moving steel, gleaming with newness, rearing up so high that the cap of the man in the turret nearly touched the top of the gate with its legend, '*Sepp Dietrich Kaserne*'.

'*Donnerwetter!*' the Vulture gasped and slapped his cane against the side of his boot.

Behind him Schulze swallowed hard and exclaimed, 'Christ on a crutch! What is it, Matzi . . ? a frigging *battleship on wheels or summat!*'

Corporal Matz was too stunned even to make an attempt to answer. Like the rest he simply stood there and gaped open-mouthed like a village yokel, as the enormous tank with its huge overhanging cannon braked to a stop with a final burst of power from its tremendous engines, and a cocky-looking one-armed SS officer sprang lightly from the turret, while the helmeted chain-dogs* who had been borne along on its deck dropped to the cobbles to form a protective screen around the monster, machine-pistols cocked and at the ready.

Smartly the one-armed officer marched up to within six paces of an astonished Vulture, who simply could not take his eyes off this massive tank, its engines still throbbing like the beat of some huge metallic heart. He snapped to attention and raised his one arm in the Hitler greeting. '*Untersturmführer* Ertz, from the SS Main Office, Berlin, *Obersturmbannführer*. Heil Hitler!'

'Heil Hitler!' the Vulture echoed the greeting without enthusiasm.

'Compliments from the Reichsführer SS Himmler, sir. I have the pleasure of handing over to you the first of your new tanks, the latest Mark VI.'

'*The latest Mark VI!*' The name flew from mouth to mouth like wildfire. '*The latest . . . Mark Six . . !*'

Smartly the one-armed officer whipped a form from inside the cuff of his sleeve, complete with pen. 'If you would be so

*Military policemen, so named because of their metal plate of office, suspended from a chain, and worn around their necks

kind, sir, may I ask you to sign for the Mark VI . . . The rest of them will follow in due course . . . The Reichsführer SS is ensuring *personally* that SS Assault Regiment Wotan will be re-equipped by the end of the month.' He smiled winningly at the Vulture.

But the latter had eyes only for the enormous tank. Numbly he took the form and fountain pen and without looking down signed the acceptance.

'Well, that's that, sir,' the young officer said cheerfully and indicated that the two Volkswagen jeeps which had now swung through the gate should take aboard himself and the escort of MPs, who withdrew, machine-pistols still held threateningly, as if they expected an assault on the top-secret tank at any moment, even here. 'I take the liberty of wishing you and your brave fellows a merry Christmas, sir!'

'Merry Christmas!' the Vulture echoed, still gazing at the tank as if he could not believe the evidence of his own eyes.

'And by the way, sir,' the younger officer called as the driver clambered out of his hatch and the throbbing metallic heart suddenly went dead, 'we've got a nickname for it . . . We call it . . . the Tiger.'

A minute later he was gone as swiftly as he had appeared and the French cyclists stalled at the gate began slowly to move off again. Doctor Claudine Louis, who was among them, took one last glance at the metal monster standing there in the middle of the parade ground, surrounded by the still awed SS men, including the tall, handsome captain she remembered from the hospital, and then she was off again, her pretty face suddenly thoughtful, very thoughtful indeed. The monster had been painted a bright white at the factory – and that could mean only one thing.

CHAPTER 4

THE VULTURE tapped the monster with his stick happily, as across the parade-ground, under the Butcher's command, a fatigue party was dragging a large Christmas tree through the snow. In two hours' time the whole of Wotan would assemble for the traditional Christmas Eve celebration. 'This much I have been able to find out from Berlin in the last hour, *meine Herren*,' he announced joyfully. 'The Tiger has still got a lot of troubles. It is still liable to break down easily. Apparently the shock we received from that damned Ivan T-34 forced our designers to hurry through the development with somewhat . . . er . . . indecent haste. However,' he raised his cane in warning to the assembled officers, 'it can be said that in both gunpower and armour the Tiger is a world-beater. With its weight – fifty-six tons – and its armour – one hundred millimetres – it is rather slow. Perhaps fifty kilometres an hour over easy terrain. However, there is not one single tank throughout the world which can outshoot it.' He fixed his monocle more firmly in his eye and rasped, 'Gentlemen, we will blast the T-34s into kingdom come with this baby!'

He let the words sink in as across the square the Butcher bellowed at the fatigue party, 'Come on, you collection of sad sacks! Get the tree inside. I'm freezing my eggs off out here. If you don't move it quick, the lot of yer will be seeing frigging Swedish curtains* for Christmas! *Dalli . . . Dalli . . .*'

Von Dodenburg sighed. The spirit of Christmas was undoubtedly foreign to Sergeant-Major Metzger's soul – if he had one. 'So it is definitely Popovland again, sir?' he queried, as the Vulture continued to gaze in naked admiration at the metal monster which had appeared so surprisingly in their midst like a Christmas gift from Mars himself.

*i.e. Prison bars

'Yes, my little bird at SS Headquarters maintains it is definitely the Eastern Front again for the whole of the IIIrd SS corps, von Dodenburg.'

'The plan, sir?' he persisted.

The Vulture shook his head and gave the younger officer a wintry smile. 'That, my dear von Dodenburg, is, if you don't mind my saying so, a very leading and indiscreet question. But I shall tell you all this much, and I must emphasize here and now that you must keep this information very much under your hats: we will not be returning to the Moscow Front. It is generally recognised now that our Führer – our *beloved* Führer,' he added quickly with a malicious smile at von Dodenburg, 'made a slight error of judgement when he launched his main attack on the Ivan capital last summer. Now, true to his inimitable genius,' he lowered his gaze with mock reverence and von Dodenburg flushed with anger, 'he has decided our next objective in Russia in the coming year will be of, let us say, more *strategic* importance than Moscow. More than that I cannot say.' He dismissed the matter and flashed a look at his wrist-watch. 'Gentlemen, I expect you in the mess at twelve hundred hours precisely. We shall all drink a glass of good French champers to toast the birth of our new baby.' He smiled and added a little sourly, 'Thereafter, unfortunately, we will have to subject ourselves to some of that cloying sentimentality which goes under the name of a German Christmas Eve. Undoubtedly we will all join hands like good little children with the men and sing "Silent Night, Holy Night" in front of the Christmas tree. What a bourgeois people we really are! *Meine Herren.*'

With that parting shot, the Vulture touched his cane to the peak of his rakishly tilted cap and departed, leaving them standing rigidly to attention for a few moments.

'Well, Kuno, what do you make of it?' Captain Dietz, one of the few veterans left from the old Wotan, asked as the two of them stamped through the snow to their own quarters to prepare for the afternoon's celebrations. Already they could hear the Wotan choir banging into '*Stille Nacht, Heilige Nacht*' as if it were a marching song of the SS and not a Christmas carol.

'Don't quite know, Dieter,' von Dodenburg answered slowly, his handsome young face showing his worry. 'Leningrad to the north perhaps, or even the Caucasus. We need that damned Popov oil down there pretty badly, of course.'

'Of course.'

They stopped as a group of excited young soldiers ran from behind the barracks throwing snowballs at each other, only to stop and freeze into the position of attention when they saw the two officers. Dietz waved for them to carry on, and off they went, shouting at each other like schoolboys, throwing snowballs once more.

'I only hope that Berlin gives us more time,' von Dodenburg said grimly. 'A lot of time. Those youngsters are as green as young corn, Dieter.'

'They will, Kuno, of course they will. My God, the work we're going to put in just to train them to work the Vulture's new toy! That alone will take weeks.'

'Suppose you're right, Dieter,' von Dodenburg conceded, his face brightening up. 'Come on then, let's get togged up to celebrate our bourgeois Christmas. But one thing is for sure, I'm not frigging well holding the Vulture's hand!'

Laughing like schoolboys just released from class after a boring lesson, they doubled to their quarters. In the shabby 18th century building opposite, the watcher in the loft put down his binoculars and with fingers that felt like clumsy sausages, began to draw the sketch of 'the Vulture's new toy'.

Candles glowed softly everywhere in the big echoing mess-hall as the choir lined up in front of the ceiling-high Christmas tree and the boy soldiers sat, arms folded as regulations required, at the long trestle-tables, faces scrubbed and glowing, waiting for the holiest moment of the German year to commence.

Standing to the rear of the hall a little way off, the Butcher and his crony the kitchen head-bull were already making arrangements concerning how much of the Christmas Eve feast rations they could sell on the Metz black market without it being noticed, while Matz and Schulze, taking discreet sips from their flatmen, eyed the bottles of wine lining the tables with some interest. As Schulze had remarked just a little earlier, 'Those greenbeaks don't need all that sauce, Matzi. A bottle o' milk would do that bunch of piss-pansies much more good.'

Now the question was how many of the rookies' bottles could they get away with for the long two-day Christmas break without having to break heads in the process? Indeed, any casual observer viewing the scene at that moment would have judged that the spirit of Christmas was sorely lacking in Wotan's NCO Corps on this Christmas Eve of 1941.

The Vulture, who was now striding into the hall followed by his officers, slapping his cane against his highly polished boot as he did so, seemed decidedly unaffected by the season's traditional mood of goodwill to all men. Nodding to the Butcher, he snapped, 'All right, let's get on with it for God's sake! And I only want *one* carol, Sergeant-Major. *Their* version of 'Silent Night' will surely do me until this time next year.'

'Yessir. Certainly sir!' the Butcher agreed hastily and drawing himself up to his full height, he bellowed, 'At the command *One*, singers will open their mouths! At the command *Two*, the lead singers will sing the first words. At the command *Three, Four*, you will commence singing.' He beamed proudly at the Vulture, obviously very pleased with himself. '*One!*'

Von Dodenburg shook his head in mock wonder, as the choir burst into '*Stille Nacht, Heilige Nacht*', and said to Deitz, 'God in Heaven, Dieter, Christmas Eve according to numbers! Where will it all end . . ?'

It ended, as it always did in SS Assault Regiment Wotan, in a drunken orgy; with the Vulture, scarlet-faced with sudden rage, slamming his cane down on the table making the Christmas tree shake alarmingly and threatening to make 'men of you rabble of wet-tails this very night'; with the Butcher and his crony, the kitchen bull staggering off with several cases of 'Old Man' to sell in Metz; and Schulze and Matz steadily drinking their way through the more reluctant recruits' beer, chortling drunkenly for reasons known only to themselves, *'Never drink water, comrades . . . cos fishes fuck in water!'*

At nine that night Captain von Dodenburg decided he had had enough of 'Christmas'. There were 'beer corpses' everywhere, laid out on the floor, propped up on the trestle-tables, awash with stale beer, slumped out in corners, mumbling drunkenly to themselves. A recruit was being sick over the Christmas tree, systematically putting out candle after candle with his vomit. He told himself it was wiser to let the men carry on to the bitter end without the presence of their officers – they deserved it after all the hard training. Together with the other officers he left. No one noticed: they were all too drunk.

It was about that time that Schulze and Matz, hopelessly drunk by now, decided there were better things on this earth than free beer and wine, namely, as Schulze put it in his own habitually delightful manner, 'hot steaming female gash'.

'A very good idea, Schulzi,' Matz agreed, managing to raise himself from his bench after two very valiant attempts. 'But where, old house? Where do we find it on Christmas Eve? Even the knocking shops are closed tonight, y'know. It's a holy day.' He almost fell into Schulze's arms. 'Pardon me, I must have stepped on a banana skin,' he apologised, looking down in bewilderment.

'Knock it off, plush-ears!' Schulze snapped. 'Can't hear meself shitting think with you mouthing it off like that. This is frogland, ain't it? They're heathens here. They know nothing about the way we Germans respect the day of the Lord.' He swept his hand around the room with its drunken soldiers, one of whom was now attempting to saw down the

Christmas tree with a table knife for reasons known only to himself. 'So everything's open, even the knocking shops!'

Matz's wizened, drunken face lit up for a moment but then the hope in his red-rimmed eyes died again almost instantly. 'We ain't got no Marie, no green rags, no *dalles*,' he objected, making the continental gesture of counting money with his thumb and forefinger.

'That's not gonna stop Frau Schulze's handsome son from dipping his wick, Matzi, on this very special day – you'd better believe it!' Schulze declared fiercely.

'But no money, no ficki-ficki!' Matz persisted.

Schulze thrust a thumb like a small, hairy pork sausage at his big chest, now well stained with beer suds. 'Frig the money! What we of Wotan want we take, comrade. Come on, Matzi. This night we either get laid or them frog mattress-pounders are going to be in for a very nasty surprise. Now listen . . .'

Thus the first of the two 'outrages' which shook both the military and civilian population of the Lorraine city that Christmas Eve of 1941 commenced . . .

With a sigh of relief the two drunken noncoms let the metal trails go and straightened up their aching backs. Opposite them on the River Moselle, clearly outlined against the half-moon, was the barge, its blackout almost perfect. But here and there chinks of yellow light indicated that it was occupied all right, as did the odd burst of masculine laughter and feminine giggles. 'Well?' Matz demanded and leaned back against the heavy object they had dragged all the way from the *Sepp Dietrich Kaserne*. 'What now?' He shivered in the night cold, a little more sober now.

'Straightforward, ain't it,' Schulze replied, eyeing the floating brothel greedily, too excited to notice the cold or the notice prominently displaced next to the gangplank which connected the barge to the towpath, advising that this was 'Officers Only' country. 'I cover you while you go up there and ask for our rights. Just ask nice and pleasant like, but let the frogs know we've plenty of muscle,' he slammed his big paw against the hard steel, 'if they decide to come it awkward. Now off with you.'

'It's allus the frigging little 'uns who have to do it,' Matz grumbled.

'Rank hath its privileges, *Corporal* Matz,' Schulze declared grandly. 'Now hoof it, *Corporal*.'

Drunkenly Matz 'hoofed it', gingerly walking up the slippery gangplank in the silver-glowing darkness, hanging on to the rail very carefully.

A dark shape detached itself from the shadows and towered above the little corporal. '*Tu veut?*' the civilian demanded, cigarette glued to his bottom lip.

'Fuck off, frog!' Matz said, remembering Schulze's advice to be 'nice and pleasant', and attempted to pass the lookout.

A hand like a small steam-shovel hit him in the chest and stopped him dead. '*Sale con!*' the Frenchman grunted.

'Hey,' Matz protested, 'you can't do that to me . . . I am a German and in the SS too. You're a conquered frog.'

'SS plays with its sausage,' the giant chortled in the thick German dialect of Lorraine. 'Ha ha!'

'What's this Marcel?' a woman's voice demanded, also in the local dialect. 'Trouble?'

'*Non, Madame* . . . Just a drunken prick . . . and a corporal at that!'

'Can't the fart read?' the woman called angrily from inside the floating brothel. 'Tell him this is Officers Only and give him his marching orders.'

'*Oui Madame*,' the giant said dutifully and turned to Matz once more. 'You heard, cloth-ears. This is officers' country here, *copain*, and we're entertaining the town major.' He chuckled throatily. 'By God, you Prussians have got some funny habits in bed. *Two* mattress-pounders with whips! What next? Now make dust, little man!'

'Make dust – *to me*,' Matz cried indignantly, 'a corporal in Wot –'

He swung wildly at the grinning civilian. Next moment he felt himself flying through the air, to land in the Moselle with a great splash.

It was then that Sergeant Schulze lost his head. In spite of his drunkenness he executed every move perfectly as he swung himself behind the 37mm anti-tank gun, threw it round effortlessly, thrust the deadly little armour-piercing shell into its gaping breech, squatted behind the sight and in the very same instant that a gasping and very sober Matz clambered out of the freezing water, pulled the firing-bar.

The night stillness was destroyed by a great roar. Scarlet flame stabbed the darkness. A bolt of hurtling white streaked towards the barge. At that range, drunk as he was, Schulze could not miss. Suddenly the barge rocked violently, as if it were sailing through a tropical storm and was not tethered to the bank of the Moselle. As if by magic a huge hole appeared in its side.

In an instant all was panic and utter confusion. Screaming women, mostly half-naked, came running onto the deck. Here and there officers, younger than the place's normal middle-aged clients who needed *Madame*'s 'special treatment' to activate their sluggish libidos, dived hurriedly over the side while there was still time. For now the floating brothel was definitely beginning to sink. Water was rapidly gushing into the hole blown in its side by the armour-piercing shell. In a few minutes she would disappear altogether.

Schulze gaped as if mesmerised at the spectacle taking place in front of his eyes, as a portly officer – the town major – staggered onto the tilting deck, hurriedly doing up his flies and crying loudly, 'Abandon ship . . . do you hear, *abandon ship!* . . . *I'm in charge . . . Abandon ship . . !*'

'Jesus H,' he whispered, awed by his own skill, all lust forgotten now, 'I've just knocked out a floating knocking shop – with one shell. Imagine that . . . *Wow!*'

'And I can imagine us being frigging well sent to Torgau for the rest of our natural lives if they frigging well catch us!' Matz urged, dripping wet, shivering all over both with cold and fear. He grabbed his big comrade's arm. 'Now let's get the fuck out of here!'

Almost reluctantly Schulze let himself be tugged away and then he too came to his senses, as the first police whistles shrilled their urgent warnings above the sound of a car engine racing towards the scene of the crime at great speed. Laughing wildly, he raced after Matz.

Behind them, the water had reached the barge's deck, where the town major, up to his knees in it, was standing rigidly to attention, fat hand raised to his brow in salute like a captain preparing to go down with his ship . . .

Von Dodenburg was bored with the place. It was crammed with German officers, faces flushed v th expensive champagne, the usual high-class whores of such establishments and a handful of well-dressed French civilians who were obviously making plenty of money out of the war. For Lorraine's steel and coal industries, supplying the Reich's war machine, were flourishing; their owners had not seen such prosperity since the boom days of World War One. Still, von Dodenburg told himself as he ordered another bottle of champagne from a supercilious waiter who obviously thought that lowly captains did not belong in such places, it was better than being back in his quarters alone, with altogether too much time to think on this lonely Christmas Eve. Much better indeed. He had been thinking too much ever since he had shot those poor wounded wretches back there on the flight from Moscow. The time for thinking had to come to an end soon; he couldn't bear much more of it. Now – soon – there had to be action again, all-consuming, violent action, and a farewell at last to introspection. He said a silent '*prosit*' to himself and swallowed a whole glass of the new bottle of champagne in one go.

It was at that very moment that von Dodenburg became involved in the kind of action he longed for, but did not expect, not on Christmas Eve at least. For just as the three-piece string orchestra launched into another one of those sentimental pieces that they knew their German masters liked on such solemn occasions, the blackout curtain at the door was roughly flung aside. A woman screamed. One of the pompous staff officers sprang to his feet in red-faced protest. A waiter dropped a tray of glasses. And then it happened

The two masked civilians, British sten-guns clasped professionally to their hips, pressed their triggers. Abruptly all was chaos as, swaying from left to right like the gun-slingers von Dodenburg had seen in cowboy films as a boy, they fired into that elegant crowd. Women screamed, officers cursed wildly. The waiters dived for cover. But there was no escaping. Systematically the two killers mowed down the guests, German and French.

Von Dodenburg, perhaps the only 'front swine' there among all the elegant, middle-aged 'rear echelon stallions', acted instinctively as the first burst of 9mm slugs ripped the length of the wall behind him, shattering the mirrors and showering his head with glass splinters. In one movement he slammed the 19th century iron table to the floor and dropped behind its shield, as yet another salvo of bullets zipped past the spot where his head had been and a woman cried out hysterically, her left breast suddenly shot to ribbons.

And there he crouched impotently, while the slaughter all around him continued, blood trickling from his newly opened wound, his arm numb and paralysed where he had slammed it into the table, so that he could not draw his pistol. It was something for which he was later grateful, for whenever one of the startled 'rear echelon stallions' tried to fight back, they were immediately slaughtered by a swift burst of fire from those two professional killers at the door.

Within five minutes it was all over. Outside there was the screech of protesting rubber. The two hooded killers nodded to each other. They swept the room with one final, terrible volley and then they were running for the car which bore them away before the police arrived, leaving the shattered room, its walls and mirrors ripped apart by their fire, to the dead and the dying.

Groggily, his head ringing but not from champagne, von Dodenburg staggered to his feet, the blood dripping steadily from his arm, and viewed the chaos, hardly aware of the voice crying urgently in his ear, 'Are you hurt, Captain . . . Please answer, are you hurt?'

Von Dodenburg shook his head, as if he were trying to wake up from a deep sleep. The face came into focus. It was dark-olive and feminine. It was the face of Doctor Claudine Louis, his own doctor, standing there dressed in white, medical bag at the ready. 'Terrorists?' he croaked, eyes wide, wild and staring. 'Were they terrorists, *Mamselle?*'

'Some would say patriots,' he thought he heard her answer, but in that total confusion, with the women screaming hysterically and the dying calling out for their mothers and their God, he was not sure. Then she was gone, satisfied he was not seriously hurt, trying to tend to the woman whose breast had been shot away.

Forty-eight hours later they became lovers . . .

CHAPTER 5

Now SS Assault Regiment Wotan worked feverishly to acquire proficiency with their specialised armoured fighting vehicle as more and more of the huge Tigers began to be delivered at the Metz railhead from the factory in far-off Augsburg. The few veterans such as Von Dodenburg, Captain Dietz, Schulze and Matz were worked off their feet from reveille to taps trying to pass on their knowledge of armoured warfare in Russia to the greenbeaks. They exercised at platoon-strength, then company, and finally battalion strength, hammering home the bitter lessons they had learned at so much cost in the East.

Von Dodenburg's approach was calm and reasoned: 'When tanks are advancing they must use their guns in what is called reconnaissance by fire. That means they must shoot at any objective which could conceal an anti-tank gun and knock it out at a range greater than that at which an anti-tank gun is effective. In other words, at a range greater than two thousand metres.'

Schulze's methods were different. With his flatman always ready in his big paw – 'my cough medicine, not what you lot think it is, piss-pansies!' – he made his points with his usual highly profane bluntness: 'If a Popov T-34 comes at yer, don't have a period. Let him have a star shell of smoke, straight at the turret. That'll blind old Ivan long enough even for a shower of shitheels like yerselves to get in an accurate shot and knock the frigger out. Now, you with the wanker's face, pretend you're a frigging Tiger and I'll pretend that I'm a frigging T-34 just breasting a hill here. What are yer frigging well gonna do . . .?'

So it went on, day after day: 'When tanks are passing or approaching hedges or walls, they should comb them with machine-guns to remove the danger from close-defence anti-tank grenades or sticky bombs . . .

'Forget the frigging mass of the T-34s. Look for a frigging one where there's some frigging Popov yo-yo waving frigging flags like a frigging boy scout cos that's the frigging command tank. Knock that frigger out and they're lost . . .

'Tankers must remember that open spaces can be passed with relative impunity as long as enough smoke is used to blind the enemy artillery spotters . . . The frigging quickest way to go to frigging heaven is to advance across frigging open ground covered by frigging A/T* fire . . .' Over and over again this terrible litany of combat – and death – was hammered home as December gave way to January; both instructors and pupils were exhausted at the end of the day, blind with fatigue, out on their feet.

Even Claudine's exciting nubile body could hardly keep von Dodenburg awake during the nights he spent with her in the old city; the usual nightly beer-bust paled for Schulze and Matz while the Butcher, although not so involved in the armoured training as the others, found the temptations of the Metz black market growing ever less attractive as the knowledge penetrated even his thick skull that the intensified training meant that they would be returning to Russia once again.

Somehow the enemy seemed to realise that too, for now Metz was subjected to almost nightly bombing raids by the RAF, and their targets were no longer Metz's thriving war industry but the 18th century caserne in the old city along the River Moselle! 'First of all, von Dodenburg, God only knows why the Tommies are helping the Reds,' the Vulture exclaimed angrily one morning, after they had spent most of the night in the cellars below the caserne. 'That drunken, toothless old sot of theirs, Churchill, hates the Reds as much as we do. Secondly, and this is a really pressing problem, von Dodenburg . . .' He stopped and called to the fatigue party clearing up the smoking mess. 'Hey, you men, there's a dead frog civvie over there. Get rid of him immediately! He's

*Anti-Tank fire

making my parade-ground look untidy. Where was I, von Dodenburg?' he asked, screwing his monocle more firmly in his right eye and glaring at the dead Frenchman as if he were making him personally responsible for getting himself killed by the RAF bomb in such an important place as Wotan's parade-ground.

'Really pressing problem, sir,' von Dodenburg answered dutifully.

'Oh, yes,' the Vulture continued as they went on past a shattered workshop. 'I almost have the impression that the Tommies know we're here and they know, too, that we are being equipped with the Reich's latest secret weapon, the Tiger.' He stopped abruptly and glared at von Dodenburg.

'How do you mean, sir?'

'Espionage! That's what I mean, von Dodenburg. *Espionage!*'

'But on the whole, sir, the population here is very pro-German. Most of the older folk speak German as their first language, indeed they were born German,' Von Dodenburg objected. 'As for the young ones, they're earning good money working for the German war industry. I can see, with all due respect, sir, no reason for the Lorraine people to wish any harm to Germany and her soldiers. After this night's bombing, I should think most of them will be anti-British.' He indicated two French employees of the barracks sprawled out in the extravagant postures of those done violently to death, their blood staining the dirty snow a dark red.

The Vulture shook his head, unconvinced. 'How then do you explain, von Dodenburg, that dreadful incident on Christmas Eve?'

'Terrorists, sir,' von Dodenburg ventured, remembering how Claudine had looked at him after she had dealt with the last of the wounded and they had both known, although not a word had been spoken, that they would soon be lovers.

'Perhaps. And where there are anti-German terrorists, there can also be spies, mark my words, von Dodenburg. From now onwards we have to be exceedingly security-conscious, *exceedingly*.' He slapped his cane angrily against his

boot, and then for the first time since they had received the
Tigers, Colonel Geier let drop a hint of what lay before them
in the future. 'You see, von Dodenburg, we have been put on
alert,' he said *sotto voce*.

'What stage, sir?' von Dodenburg asked excitedly.

'Three! So that means Berlin can order us to move *eastwards*
within forty-eight hours and I'm not having some damned
frog spy signalling the Reds that we are coming. No sir!' And
with another angry slap of his cane he was gone, marching
briskly across the littered parade-ground in his absurd baggy
riding breeches, leaving von Dodenburg staring after him
thoughtfully. In forty-eight short hours they could be gone
again . . .

In the second weekend of January Captain Dietz, the
veteran, disappeared. At first no one was unduly alarmed
when he did not return to his quarters on Saturday night. In
the officers' mess the greenbeaks, lazily drinking their Sunday
morning 'nigger sweat' and enjoying the luxury of not having
to rush out for another day's hard training, nudged each
other knowingly. 'Found himself some nice juicy, willing frog
skirt no doubt,' they said. 'The lucky dog! I could do with
some of that,' they boasted. 'Got so much ink in my fountain
pen, I don't know who to write to first . . .'

When, however, Captain Dietz did not return for the
traditional mess Sunday lunch, where it was the Vulture's
habit to quiz his officers on the state of training and expound
his own unorthodox ideas on tank tactics, the handful of
veterans began to become worried. 'It's not like him, Kuno,'
the Pill, the grey-haired regimental surgeon, whispered
behind his hand to von Dodenburg as at the head of the table
the Vulture illustrated his method of attacking high ground
with the aid of several salt-cellars and a champagne bottle.
'He's too old a fox to lose his head over a skirt. Even you with
your . . . er . . . pleasant little relationship with my charming
colleague,' he beamed at the young officer, 'you would not

allow yourself to miss one of our commander's weekly lectures, would you?'

'Pill, she's on duty today,' von Dodenburg answered, smilingly. 'Besides, after last week's schedule, I'm only too glad to put my feet up.'

'No stamina, my boy, that's what it is,' the Pill joked. 'At your age I used to be a stallion. Insatiable . . .'

It was at two that afternoon that the Vulture received the terrible news from the military hospital that Dietz had been found – dead and mutilated. Would he like to see for himself? The Vulture would.

Even the Vulture was shocked when the *Oberarzt* drew back the sheet to reveal the dead officer's body stretched out naked on the slab. He nodded to an ashen-faced Claudine holding the check board in a hand that von Dodenburg noted trembled ever so slightly.

'Multiple head injuries,' she read, while the other stared in horror at that terrible sight on the slab, 'which look as if they have been made with a blunt instrument, perhaps a hammer.' She swallowed hard and von Dodenburg just caught himself from hurrying across to her in time; she really was moved by what had been done to his dead comrade. 'Both eyes have been excised. Clumsy, unprofessional work . . . perhaps carried out with a . . . penknife.'

'The swine . . . the swine . . !' the Vulture hissed through gritted teeth, the knuckles of his hand holding the cane white with suppressed anger.

'The initials "SS" carved on his chest – superficial wounds, and' – Claudine's voice almost broke as the sad-faced old *Oberarzt* drew back the sheet completely to reveal poor Dietz's cruelly tortured loins under the harsh white light from the ceiling – 'Captain Dietz's testicles and scrotum have been removed.' She turned away and swayed as if she might faint at any moment. Hastily the Pill caught her and said, 'My dear Colleague, please contain yourself.'

She nodded weakly and looked at the *Oberarzt*. He shook his head as if there was nothing more to be said and then slowly, gently, covered the corpse once more, as a heavy, brooding silence filled the room, broken only by the steady metallic tick of the clock on the white-painted wall.

Suddenly, startlingly, the Vulture slammed his cane down against the table, eyes blazing with fury. 'From now on we take hostages!' he barked. 'For every German soldier who is murdered by these heartless wretches, I will personally see that ten French citizens are executed. I will *not* have my regiment destroyed in this manner. *Himmelherrgott*, the French will learn with whom they are dealing from this day onwards! *Fire will fight fire!*'

Von Dodenburg flashed a quick look at Claudine, but she avoided his gaze and then he too was stalking out after the Vulture who was muttering wildly to himself, his ugly face dominated by that beak of a nose, mad with rage . . .

Thus it was, as the first important, pompous General Staff officers with the red stripe of their calling down the sides of their elegant breeches began to appear at the Wotan's headquarters carrying their top secret documents from Berlin in briefcases chained to their wrists, that the terror came to Metz. A corporal from one of the *Wehrmacht* supply companies was found stabbed to death in a whore's bed in the old city. The Vulture overruled the town major's protests and had the first ten civilians his patrol encountered in the same area arrested and shot. That same night as the cable arrived from Himmler congratulating him on 'the vigour of your counter-measures to stamp out these terrorist swine', a grenade was flung through the gate of the *Sepp Dietrich Kaserne* by a kid speeding by on a bicycle, wounding two of the now heavily armed sentries. At dawn the following morning ten cyclists were rounded up on their way to work and shot dead at the very same spot where the bomb had been thrown. Fire *was* fighting fire and the blaze was getting ever higher . . .

One week after the terror had started in the ancient Lorraine city, the Mayor himself, dressed in a frock coat with

the sash of his office around his portly chest but also wearing
the Iron Cross he had won in the Kaiser's army in the Old
War, made his appearance at Wotan's HQ. He was polite,
but firm. 'Colonel Geier, you will achieve nothing by these
measures,' he declared without any preliminaries, 'save the
alienation of a population nearly one hundred per cent
behind Germany's war effort. My people aren't terrorists, but
in due course they will become terrorists if you continue on
your present course.'

Even the Vulture was impressed by the old man's
outspokenness.

'But somebody – some civilian – must be killing my
soldiers,' he protested a little feebly.

The old man stroked his beard, suddenly hesitant. 'Of
course,' he countered, 'that is true. But it is not my people. I
am prepared to put my hand in the fire for them.'

'Then who is it?'

The old man looked glum. 'Herr Geier, Metz has always
employed labour from elsewhere. We have never had
sufficient numbers in Metz to keep the factories running.
Hence we have always imported workers from other parts of
France, even from the Colonies. Undoubtedly you will find
your . . . er . . . terrorists among them. My advice to you, sir,
is to start looking for the culprits among our southern labour,
especially those from the *Midi* and *Provence*. They have always
been notorious *franc-tireurs* in that region. Good day to you,
sir.' He seized his top hat and was gone, leaving the Vulture
looking thoughtfully at von Dodenburg, an idea beginning to
unfurl itself like some evil snake in his perverted mind.

Two days after the indignant Senior Mayor of Metz had
lodged his protest with the Vulture, the SS Assault Regiment
Wotan had its first breakthrough. One of the morning
fatigue party, whose job it was to 'shovel shit', i.e. remove the
effluent from the Regiment's waterless 'thunderboxes',
disappeared. Six hours after he had done so, he had made his

reappearance propped up against the wall opposite the main gate smoking a cigarette, or so it appeared, with *'merde à SS'* written across his young forehead in human faeces, and very dead, with his throat cut from ear to ear.

Naturally the Vulture had gone into his usual act, slapping the desk with his cane, threatening tremendous reprisals, cursing the French for the treacherous ungrateful swine they were, until a pale-faced, agitated Pill announced, 'You know, sir, I think I know where they did for the poor chap!'

'*What?*' the assembled officers had exclaimed as one, staring at the ancient surgeon with his lined, worried face and white hair. 'What did you say?'

'Look at his boots,' was the surgeon's response. 'You don't see red mud like that around here in Metz.' He took his pocket-knife and excised a section of dark earth from the dead youth's right boot. 'There's only one place you'll get red dirt like that on your dice-beakers.'*

'And where is that?' the Vulture demanded harshly.

'Verdun.'

'*Verdun?*' half a dozen voices echoed.

'Yes,' the Vulture snapped, 'how would you know that, Pill?'

'Sixteen, sir,' he answered, a proud little smile on his old face in spite of the dead youth spread out in front of him on the slab.

'*Himmel, Arsch und Wolkenbruch!*' von Dodenburg exclaimed incredulously. 'Even you cannot be *that* old, Pill!'

The surgeon looked at him. 'Oh yes I can. I was there too you know, as an officer-cadet under a certain Captain Paulus of the Leib Regiment.'

'You mean Paulus the general?' the Vulture snapped.

'That's right, sir. Well, sir, Verdun's the only place you find red earth like that around here. We used to say it was coloured red by the blood of our brave soldiers who died there in their thousands. In Captain Paulus's battalion alone, sir,

*German Army slang for jackboots

we lost . . .' The Pill faltered to a stop. The Vulture was no longer interested in his memories of that great blood-letting in the Old War. Like the rest he waited.

Finally the Vulture spoke. 'I think Pill here has got it right. Assuming that the general populace of Metz is pro-German, as everyone seems to be saying, then it would be too dangerous to slaughter my poor fellows in the town itself. Someone might well betray the terrorists to the authorities. So somewhere in the country would be a much more suitable spot.'

'Verdun in particular, sir,' von Dodenburg said. 'My father fought there, sir, so I too had occasion to go to the place. It is a particularly lonely place these days.'

The Pill nodded his agreement.

'A few odd traces of the villages that were abandoned back in Sixteen and the ruins of the forts – Douaumont, Vaux and the like. In short, sir, an ideal place for terrorists to do their work without being disturbed.'

The Vulture thought for a moment, stroking his monstrous beak of a nose, and then he made his decision. 'Assuming that that old battlefield is the site of the terrorists' activities and that they will return to the place in due course, this is what we are going to do . . .'

CHAPTER 6

ON THAT same afternoon that the Vulture made his minor decision to set a trap for a handful of unknown terrorists, a thousand kilometres away in his remote East Prussian headquarters, his Führer Adolf Hitler made a *major* decision: one of overwhelming proportions that would soon involve SS Assault Regiment Wotan in a titanic life and death struggle.

Facing his top army commanders in that wooden, spartanly furnished hut which served as his operations room, the only sound from outside the steady tread of the SS sentries on the gravel paths, he stroked his alsatian bitch Blondi and waited till they began to show the first sign of nerves and he knew he had gained their attention. As always he commenced his briefing with one of his usual dramatic statements, well calculated to shock, startle, anger his generals. '*Meine Herren*,' he rasped, 'the winter battle in Russia is drawing to its close. The enemy has suffered very heavy losses in men and material. In his anxiety to exploit what seemed like initial successes around Moscow he has spent during this winter the bulk of his reserves marked for spring operations.'

Only Keitel, the immensely tall, wooden-faced Chief-of-Staff, nodded his approval of the Führer's announcement, but then he had always been a toady; the other senior generals reserved their judgement and waited.

'It is therefore obvious, gentlemen, that the time has come to strike,' Hitler continued easily, as if the Greater German *Wehrmacht* had not already lost a half a million soldiers in the East. 'As soon as weather and ground conditions permit, the German forces, which are now obviously superior, must seize the initiative again and impose their will upon the enemy. The aim of the *Wehrmacht, meine Herren*,' Hitler gave his top commanders that penetrating look which they all knew so well, and feared too, for it always heralded problems – and worse, 'is to destroy what manpower the Soviets have left and deprive them as far as possible of their vital military-economic potential. Now where can that aim best be achieved? *Jodl!*'

Colonel-General Jodl, his pale-faced, cunning-eyed Chief-of-Operations stepped forward smartly and positioned himself in front of the huge map of the Eastern Front which decorated one wall of the wooden hut. Like Keitel, he too was a lackey, but he was a clever one and the top brass now pricked up their ears. Jodl would not lecture them like Hitler; he would give a military-efficient estimate of the situation at the front.

'While adhering in general to the overall plan of the campaign, gentlemen,' he snapped, 'we shall now hold back temporarily on the central front.'

Most of his listeners breathed an inner sigh of relief. That meant no more precious German lives would be lost trying to take Moscow, a prestige object that had no military value.

'Instead, all available forces will be concentrated for the main operation in the southern sector. Its objective will be the annihilation of the enemy on the Don and the subsequent gaining of the oilfields in the Caucasian region and the crossing of the Caucasus itself.' Jodl tapped the map with his pale hand, the nails well-manicured as befitted a senior officer who wore the stripe of the Greater General Staff on his elegant breeches. 'Two army groups will form a huge pair of pincers. The northern jaw of the pincers – here – will advance from the Kursk-Kharkov area down the Middle Don to the south-east. The southern jaw will drive rapidly eastwards from the Taganrog area – here. The two jaws will meet west of Stalingrad, enclosing the bulk of the Soviet forces between Donets and Don. Those Soviet forces will be annihilated. Thereafter, we will advance into the Caucasus and capture the Russian oilfields. That is the plan, gentlemen.' He stepped back immediately, his cunning face showing absolutely no emotion, revealing nothing of his own attitude to this tremendous new offensive which entailed liquidating a Russian army nearly a million strong, capturing the fortified

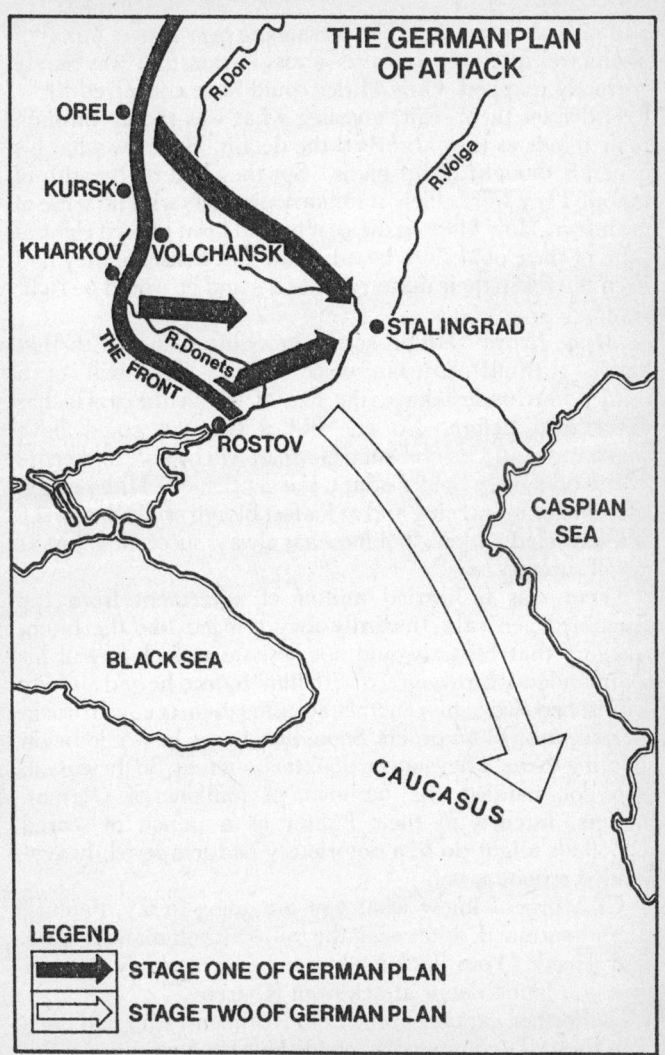

THE GERMAN PLAN
OF ATTACK

OREL

KURSK

KHARKOV VOLCHANSK

R.Don

R.Volga

THE FRONT

R.Donets

STALINGRAD

ROSTOV

CASPIAN
SEA

BLACK SEA

CAUCASUS

LEGEND

STAGE ONE OF GERMAN PLAN

STAGE TWO OF GERMAN PLAN

city of Stalingrad and then advancing over twelve hundred kilometres into the Caucasus across terrain that was barely correctly mapped. Only Hitler could have conceived it!

Hitler let them wait, guessing what was racing through their minds as they absorbed the details. He knew what his generals thought of his plans, but they had no breadth of vision. They were efficient military plodders with no sense of grandeur. How often in the past he had been proved right in spite of their objections based on all that nonsense they had been taught in their military schools – and he would be right again.

'*Meine Herren!*' He broke the brooding silence with that harsh, guttural Austrian voice of his. 'This will be a tremendous undertaking, the like of which the world has never seen before. No one but a German could have conceived it and no one but a German will be able to execute it. It is bold, very bold, I admit. But gentlemen,' Hitler raised a forefinger in warning and at his feet Blondi cringed, as if she half-expected a blow, 'boldness has always succeeded, just as it will succeed now!'

There was a hurried mutter of agreement from the assembled generals. Inwardly they cringed like the bitch, knowing that Hitler would not hesitate to sack any of his commanders who disagreed with him. Indeed he had already imprisoned two of his generals, accusing them of cowardice in the execution of his orders. Soon, they knew, he would begin shooting them. They had no doubts about that. So these men, who commanded the destinies of millions of German soldiers, listened to their Führer as a bunch of scared schoolkids might do to a notoriously bad-tempered, heavy-handed schoolmaster.

'Of course, I know what you are going to say, Paulus,' Hitler continued, addressing the tall, lean commander of his Sixth Army. 'Your flank is going to be increasingly exposed once you launch your attack from Kharkov.'

The former captain in the Leib Regiment, who had once been the Pill's commander, nodded his head warily. All the time the Führer had been speaking, he had been worrying about exactly that aspect of the coming attack.

'You are probably concerned,' Hitler went on, 'that the enemy might launch a counter-attack – say from the area of Volchansk. But I can assure you here and now, *categorically*, Colonel-General, that you have nothing to fear, because I shall ensure that you will receive perhaps the best troops still available in Germany today to guard that flank.' He lowered his voice to give his words the fullest significance so that his high-ranking listeners had to strain to catch his final words. 'And those troops will be armed with the latest and finest tank in the world, an armoured fighting vehicle which is virtually unstoppable – the Tiger!'

'And those troops are, *mein Führer?*' Paulus asked, impressed but not yet convinced.

Adolf Hitler beamed at the tall officer whom he would both make field marshal and publicly disown before this terrible year of 1942 was over. 'Can you not guess, *Herr General?* No other unit could do the job but *Colonel Geier's SS Assault Regiment Wotan!*'

The brass was impressed. But suddenly and inexplicably, Blondi threw back her snout and started to howl. Her master fussed with her but she simply would not be stopped. A little angrily, Hitler called for an orderly to take her outside, where she continued with that strange banshee-like keening: a kind of animal mourning – but for what?

Listening in the middle of that suddenly silent room, the tall commander of the German Sixth Army felt the small hairs at the back of his neck stand on end. Abruptly he was overcome by a feeling of foreboding. With the sudden, total clarity of a revelation, he knew things were going to go wrong . . .

Sergeant Schulze, crouched next to Matz on the cold windy heights of that old slaughter-ground of Verdun, felt a similar strange sense of foreboding as the light started to give and long shadows began to slip silently, like great black crows, across the desolate, shattered terrain.

It was nearly three decades now since over 700,000 Germans and Frenchmen had died on these heights, but still nothing grew up here save stunted gorse bushes and shrubs. Even the grass was sparse and uneven. It was as if God himself has ordained that nothing should grow here again to cover the terrible scars inflicted upon His earth by crazy men.

Schulze was not an imaginative man, but even he felt that there was something spooky about this old battlefield, with shattered concrete bunkers, shell-pitted earth and tangled, rusted barbed-wire everywhere. It was a place still inhabited by those long-dead soldiers in their field-grey and horizon-blue. Somehow living men should feel themselves strangers and unwanted here. Verdun belonged to the ghosts. He shivered dramatically and, crouching next to him on the roof of the fort, Matz whispered anxiously, 'Anything wrong, Schulzi?'

'No,' Schulze hissed back almost angrily, 'just a louse ran over me liver that's all.'

Kneeling next to the steel cupola of the retractable gun turret on top of the old French fort, surveying the plain below with his night glass, von Dodenburg commanded curtly, 'Keep the noise down to a roar, you two rogues. We don't want to give our position away.'

'Sir,' Schulze answered dutifully and fell silent, though he kept look ng over his right shoulder a little anxiously at regular intervals, as if he half-expected a line of ghost-infantry to be advancing on the fort down below, as they had once done in that terrible battle – to be slaughtered in their hundreds of thousands.

Von Dodenburg, busy with his glasses, felt the eerie chillness of the place too. With the wind whistling through the gorse and night descending on the deserted plantations, it was not somewhere he would have liked to traverse on his own. This place was the nearest thing to a desert in Europe: a desert where one might get lost for ever and die forgotten, just

like the three skeletons they had come across as they sneaked
through the labyrinth of firecuts to take up their positions: two
stretcher-bearers and the wounded man they had been
carrying, all three killed by the same shell and forgotten there
in the wilderness thirty or more years ago.

What folly and what waste there had been in that year.
Even the stupendous courage and spirit of self-sacrifice of
both the French and the German soldiers could not hide that,
von Dodenburg told himself as he searched the plain. This
place was peopled with ghosts, the spirits of men condemned
to death like cattle to satisfy the monstrous ambitions and
vanities of high-ranking generals, safely tucked away in their
châteaux far from the murder, the carnage, the instant death.
Suddenly von Dodenburg forgot his bitter memories, passed
on to him by his father, the general, and focused his night
glasses hurriedly.

A line of dark figures was plodding slowly and cautiously
down the fire-break to the right of the little fort! They were
spread out, whoever they were, like some 1916 infantry
patrol, weapons at the ready, tensed for the first startling
rattle of a machine-gun. But these were no ghosts, he
realised, his brain racing, the danger pumping adrenaline
into his bloodstream: these were the enemy; the ruthless
killers they had come to eliminate!

'Stand by,' he hissed, ducking behind the rusting steel
cupola with its surface gnarled by the scars of shell-bursts from
that old war. 'Here they come . . . fire-break at two o'clock!'

The men, veterans and greenbeaks, gripped their weapons
more firmly in hands that were suddenly wet with sweat, eyes
narrowed to slits as they tried to penetrate the faintly glowing
gloom. Now the strangers were less than two hundred
metres away and there was no mistaking the fact that they
were armed men up to no good; the very way they moved in
cautious, hesitant silence indicated that. These were definitely
the terrorists! The Pill had been right.

'Hold your fire till I give you the command,' von
Dodenburg ordered as the terrorists came to a halt right in

the middle of the fire-break, faces white blurs turned up to the darkening sky. For a minute von Dodenburg was puzzled. What were they doing standing out in the open like that? Suddenly he heard the faint drone of the plane coming from the west and as the terrorists split up and began lighting the pile of old timber stacked in the centre of the fire-break it dawned on him. Of course! Not only was this deserted battlefield an ideal place to carry out their murder and mayhem, but it was also the best spot in the whole region for receiving the arms they needed from London. Not even courting couples would venture into this haunted wilderness. The terrorist band were obviously going to take an air-drop of clandestine weapons!

Swiftly, as the noise of airplane engines grew ever louder, he explained to the men of his patrol what was going to happen, noting as he did so the glitter of excitement in their eyes. 'We'll collar the lot of them,' he ended, 'but we want that plane too, if we can get it. I promise the lot of you free beer for a week if we knock it out of the sky. From Munich!'

'On, sir,' Schulze hissed eagerly. 'I'd shoot ten of the Tommy shits out of the sky for free suds . . . with my shitting glassy orbits closed at that. All right Matzi, on yer frigging knees.'

Obediently the little corporal did as he was told, as hastily Schulze picked up the heavy MG 42 machine-gun and rested it across the other man's shoulder which now formed a convenient rest for the weapon. Swiftly he adjusted the sight then waited. The sound of powerful engines was almost upon them now, echoing and re-echoing around the circle of low hills.

Von Dodenburg nodded his approval. 'Wait till we have them busy with the para-containers,' he commanded, 'and then let them have it with all you've got. I don't want any of them escaping into the undergrowth. It would be taking our lives in our hands to go after them into that wilderness. *Klar?*'

There was a murmur of agreement from the men, their nerves tingling electrically with tension, as the still unseen English plane started to come lower and the men on the ground twisted and turned their heads, searching the night sky for the first sign of the plane.

With startling suddenness a red light, followed almost instantly by a green one, began to wink off and on in the sky and by straining their eyes they could now make out the dark, ugly shape of a four-engined bomber, its fuselage obviously painted pitch-black to blend into the darkness.

'There it is,' Schulze whispered excitedly and swung the machine-gun round.

'Hey, frigging well watch it!' Matz grunted. 'You nearly had my neck off there.'

'Wouldn't make no difference to you, arsehole. You ain't got nothing in the upper storey as it is.'

'Piss in the wind!' Matz snorted.

But Schulze had no time now for what he thought was witty, sophisticated repartee. His whole attention was concentrated on the bomber which was coming lower and lower, his big forefinger curling slowly around the trigger of the MG 42.

The plane was directly above the little group of Frenchmen standing around the beacon. Now von Dodenburg could see some sort of movement at the plane's left side. Obviously a hatch of some kind had been opened. They were preparing to drop their supplies. Up front in the cockpit the pilot would be throttling back almost to stalling speed to ensure that none of the precious supplies overshot the dropping zone. It was now or never. Even the poorest shot among the greenbeaks could hardly miss now; the French swine were clearly outlined a stark black against the leaping flames. Von Dodenburg hesitated no longer. '*FEUER!*' he cried at the top of his voice.

His men needed no urging. At once a tremendous volley of small-arms fire erupted from the top of the fort. Tiny red flames, as thick as a swarm of bees, flew towards the surprised French. In that same instant, Schulze opened up with his MG 42. At a thousand rounds per minute, the gleaming yellow cartridge cases rattling to the ground, a stream of tracer hurried up towards the bomber like gleaming ping-pong balls. At that range Schulze could not miss. Great lumps of suddenly glistening silver metal began to fall from the plane. It staggered visibly, as if it had just run into an invisible wall. 'Great crap on the Christmas tree!' Schulze yelled crazily, carried away by the wild excitement of the moment. 'It's gonna be free Munich suds for ever!'

Smoke started to stream from the English plane's port engine. The unknown pilot fought desperately to keep his aircraft in the sky. Bravely the dispatchers started to push their cargo overboard before it was too late. Little parachutes began to crack open with a burst of white silk. But to no avail!

Below, the trapped Frenchmen were being slaughtered by that cruelly massed fire. And the men of Wotan had no mercy. They had seen what had happened to their slaughtered comrades. This terrible night they were paying the French back.

With a last great despairing howl, the British plane came hurtling from the sky. It struck the earth so that the concrete of the fort trembled and shivered with the shock. For a few unbelievable moments the pilot somehow managed to keep control as the plane skated along the earth with its undercarriage snapped, throwing up a huge wake of mud and grass. Suddenly the left wing slammed into a tree and was neatly sliced off. It careened round wildly. An engine fell off. Then another. There was the cloying stench of escaping petrol. And then it happened, as it had to happen. The shattered plane erupted in a great searing violet sheet of flame in the same moment that the few surviving Frenchmen threw away their weapons, crying piteously *'camarade!'* and von Dodenburg, sickened with the slaughter began yelling, 'Cease fire . . . *In three devils' name, cease fire . . !'*

CHAPTER 7

'THEY SANG, of course, *meine Herren*,' the ancient fat Gestapo man in his creaking green leather coat said easily, 'like sweet little yeller canaries.' He laughed, showing a mouthful of gold teeth, and took another drag at his cheap cigar, dipping the end in the glass of cognac the Vulture had offered him before he did so. 'They allus do with old Heinz. I've got my ways, you know, gentlemen.' He clenched a knobbly fist to make his meaning quite clear.

Von Dodenburg frowned. So did the Vulture, but for other reasons. The fat Gestapo inspector was so hopelessly working class, with his gold teeth and cheap cigar. But he kept his peace. *Kommissar* Heinz had solved the problem of the terrorists, it seemed. Now he could move the Regiment without any more trouble for that particular quarter.

'*Jawohl, ja*,' the Gestapo man continued, obviously very pleased with the results of his last twenty-four hours' work since he had arrived from Berlin to interrogate the prisoners von Dodenburg had taken. 'Back in the *Prinz Albrecht Strasse*,* the boys joke that old Heinz could make even an Egyptian mummy talk.'

'So, Herr Heinz,' the Vulture asked, wishing obviously to be rid of this fat, vulgar policeman, 'you are sure you have rounded up the whole gang of them here in Metz now?'

'Yessir. Nothing escapes old Heinz's lynx-eye, as the boys in the *Prinz Albrecht Strasse* say. Old Heinz bagged the lot of them, that's for sure. Professors, teachers, clerks, the whole lot of them bourgeois pseudo-intellectuals who supported the real killers – with their traps, of course. That kind don't like blood,' he chuckled throatily, his fat jowls wobbling and took another drag at his cheap cigar. 'Except for the couple of

*Gestapo HQ in Berlin

bone-menders we took, one of them a frog woman. No, there's no flies on old Heinz!'

Von Dodenburg looked alarmed and opened his mouth to ask something, but the Vulture beat him to it. 'They will be shot, of course, *Herr Kommissar?*' he snapped.

'Of course, sir. The town major has arranged a firing squad. He didn't want to bother you with it. There seems to be some sort of flap on, or so a little bird has told me.' He looked keenly at the Vulture, whose record he had perused before he left Berlin, and told himself once again the snooty SS colonel was damned lucky he hadn't ended up behind Swedish curtains himself. What with that business with the teenage kid in Berlin just before the war and the others since. But the Russians would probably knock the wind and piss out of Colonel Geier before long; they might even do for him for good – and it wouldn't be too great a loss for the world either.

'Excellent,' the Vulture said and Heinz reached automatically for his hat.

'Then I'll be going, gentlemen,' he said, wishing they would ask him to stay for another glass of cognac, but knowing they wouldn't; he was not good enough for them. Inside he chuckled: *he* would survive this shitting war, they, the fine gentlemen of the SS, *wouldn't*.

'I'll see you to the gate,' Von Dodenburg heard himself saying, trying not to see the look of surprise on the Vulture's ugly mug. 'Come on, *Herr Kommissar*, this way.'

Surprised too, Heinz let himself be led out of the office into the courtyard packed with soldiers in fatigues manhandling crates, stacking bedrolls and extra fuel cans on the great steel monsters and loading ammunition, while red-faced NCOs marched back and forth issuing orders, their breath fogging on the cold winter air. 'You're moving, sir, I see,' Heinz ventured.

Von Dodenburg nodded, his mind on other things, automatically saluting the NCOs and nodding encouragingly to the junior officers supervising the loading. 'May I ask you a question, Herr Heinz?' he asked at last, as they reached the gate with its rigid, helmeted sentries.

'Fire away, sir,' Heinz answered. 'Anything old Heinz knows, he tells. Well almost,' he added with a knowing throaty chuckle.

'The bone-mender . . . er. . . the doctor you rounded up. Remember?'

'Yessir, I remember.'

'May I ask her name, *Herr Kommissar?*' von Dodenburg asked lamely, handsome young face suddenly tense.

Heinz's heart leapt. So this was the one, this arrogant high-faluting aristocrat: this was the one she had let fuck her in order to find out the information the Reds in Moscow wanted. It had taken a lot to get her to sing; tough she certainly was. They had given her the water, the electricity, the thumb-screws, the whole works, until her body had been black and blue, her eyes closed, her nipples swollen from the electrodes like ripe plums, the whole of her pubic hair burned off. In the end the oldest trick of all had worked, surprisingly enough. He had ripped open his flies, while his colleagues had laughed their heads off, and pulled out his old salami, waving it in front of her beaten face, saying harshly, 'Well then, if you're not prepared to talk, *Fräulein*, old Heinz'll be forced to try something else. Spread her out on the operating table, lads!'

That had done it. She had screamed hysterically, as if she had never seen a piece of male salami before, and had begun to babble as if she would never stop again. The whys, the wherefores, the how, the whos. God in heaven, she must have kipped with half the officers in Metz to obtain the info that the Moscow Ivans so desperately needed. Only one had she really loved and never attempted to pump: an SS officer and even now as she whimpered in front of him, her naked shoulders heaving with emotion, she had not been prepared to tell him his name. But he knew it now, as he always knew everything in the end. *It was Captain Kuno von shitting Dodenburg of the élite SS Assault Regiment Wotan!*

He stopped suddenly and faced a waiting von Dodenburg.

'The name, Captain von Dodenburg, do you really want to know?' Gently he laid a paternal hand on the young officer's sleeve. 'If I were you, I would not bother to ask. Who knows what . . . er. . . *complications* it could result in. You understand?' He looked significantly at von Dodenburg. 'After all, she was associated with the terrorists and indirectly had the blood of your own soldiers on her pretty hands.'

Von Dodenburg simply stood there, facing the old cop, the two of them frozen thus like two characters at the end of a second-rate 19th century melodrama.

In the end *Kommissar* Heinz dropped his hand from von Dodenburg's arm and with a tug of his heavy green trilby and a gruff '*Auf Wiedersehen*' he was limping through the gate, von Dodenburg's gaze fixed with a look of almost passionate longing on his leather-clad back. Abruptly, however, he stopped and turned, a sly grin on his old face. 'Oh, one thing old Heinz forgot to tell you, Captain, she – the woman in question – hanged herself in her cell early this morning. Goodbye, sir . . .' Then he was gone.

Snowflakes fell gently, almost sadly. They would be the last of this winter in France. Already the crocuses were thrusting their white heads through the snow outside the big echoing station. Now the sounds of the great Lorraine city were beginning to quieten as its prosperous citizens settled down for another night. Here and there the searchlights flicked their icy-white fingers across the heavens searching for the English, that is if they were fools enough to fly on a night like this.

Outside on the pavement, the soldiers crowding the wet platform waiting for the midnight departure of the long train to the east could hear the steady tramp of the chaindogs.* They were there to seal off the area from prying eyes and perhaps to stop any of the Wotan troopers who might have

*Military Police

second thoughts at the very last moment. But this night there would be no deserters. The men had no heart for anything. Even the drunks among Wotan's NCO Corps could raise not much more than a sad subdued laugh at the tired old jokes and boasts. The *skat* players, already occupying their seats, played their cards without the usual noise and good-natured curses that normally accompanied the game. All was moody sombreness, as if for the first time they all realised exactly where they were going – and for what.

Schulze and Matz, who were already well-oiled, crowded near to the pot-bellied iron stove, though the best place was still unoccupied; that was reserved for the Butcher. Both had equipped themselves well for the long journey: carefully stowed in the fresh straw of their bed spaces at the side of the goods wagon there was a line of bottles, each one labelled for the time and the day of its use: '1M', '1N', '2M', '2N'* etc. Hanging from nails knocked into the wooden wall above their bed spaces were sides of smoked bacon and French salami and a netful of beer which they would drink for breakfast. And to provide for intellectual entertainment there was a well-thumbed pile of *La Vie Parisienne* and other pornographic magazines, each clearly stencilled with the warning in red ink: '*STOLEN FROM SERGEANT SCHULZE – DANGER!!!*'

But despite their comfy billet within one metre of the stove, and the fact that they had still lice-free straw for the long journey and ample supplies of liquid refreshment, the two comrades were also infected by the mood of the hour. The conversation was limited to grunts, farts (for there had been generous portions of green-pea soup for supper) and the occasional polite request to 'toss over the fucking bottle, you greedy barn-shitter!' They knew only too well where they were going and what was waiting there for them and the mass of greenbeaks – *death*.

Only the Vulture seemed happy that last night in Metz before the world changed for SS Wotan and Germany.

*German for 'First Morning', 'First Afternoon', 'Second Morning', 'Second Afternoon' etc.

'Stalingrad,' he kept whispering to himself, savouring the name of the Russian town, breaking it down into syllables: '*Sta-lin-grad!*' It had a pleasant sound to it, he told himself, as if Berlin had been called 'Hitler-city'. Surely any commander who materially aided the capture of the city which bore the Russian dictator's name would receive his general's stars at the end of the campaign? *Surely!*

But already Captain Kuno von Dodenburg knew, as he stood at the far end of the long platform staring out at the dark, spiky shape of the city he would never see again, that SS Assault Regiment Wotan would never reach Stalingrad. They had been betrayed already; the Popovs knew they were coming, that was what it had been all about. He stared at the infinite blue wash of the night sky, studded with its myriad silver stars, and shivered at the uncertainty and horror of what was to come, as from the long troop train the greenbeaks began to 'baa' in unison like lambs being led to the slaughter – and impatient to meet the executioner's block. 'BAA . . . BAA . . . BAA . . .'

Thus SS Assault Regiment Wotan went to Russia for the second time . . .

PART TWO

Storm Attack

'With very great heroism they struggled long and desperately against their own fate and it was the bravest among them who were betrayed most cruelly.'

Peter Bamm: [*The invisible flag*]

CHAPTER 1

OUTSIDE THE great palace, with its golden, onion-shaped towers, it was snowing again. The great wet flakes drifting down muted the stamp of thousands of jackbooted feet, as yet another division of infantry marched through Moscow to encourage the civilians to further efforts on its way to the front. Now and again the sound of a tram penetrated that great gloomy hall. But that was all. Even the marshals, squat, broad-faced men seemingly weighed down by the heavy golden epaulettes that had been re-introduced from the old Czarist Army were silent, and perhaps a little apprehensive, casting furtive glances at the Dictator at the far end of the room, wondering what might be going on in his mind at this moment.

Stalin's worn, leathery face revealed nothing. He slumped in his thronelike chair, which had once belonged to the Czar he had helped to murder so long before, sucking his cold pipe, dark eyes veiled, giving away nothing. To any casual observer he might well have been dead, save for the soft rise and fall of his chest. 'Old Leather Face', as those one-time Czarist NCOs who were now his marshals called him behind his back, was brooding, and when the ruler of the Soviet Union brooded, it boded no good for someone.

Only Comrade Beria, the Chief of the dreaded Secret Police, with his schoolmaster's pince-nez and icy cold eyes, seemed unaffected by the mood of this day and place. He laughed and joked quite loudly with the hunchbacked civilian who was Stalin's secretary. But then Comrade Beria was a Georgian like Stalin himself. He had a special relationship with the dictator. It was said that he procured for Old Leather Face too, those 'green fruit', as Beria called the virginal girls snatched off the streets of Moscow at night and beaten bloody with the knout until he, Beria, was sexually stimulated enough to be able to rape them. Both of them, these Georgians, were monsters, the waiting marshals told themselves: monsters who would have a marshal of the Soviet Union slaughtered as easily as those unfortunate girls who disappeared afterwards into the cellars of the NKVD* never to reappear.

Outside the muted stamp of marching feet continued. The trams jingled. Stalin sucked his empty pipe, and life seemed to have stopped inside the Kremlin. Here and there a marshal dabbed his brow with a handkerchief soaked in cheap eau de Cologne, as if he were about to faint. Then tension began to mount. What in the devil's name was going on in Old Leather Face's mind? *Boshe moi!* The uncertainty and this damned waiting was enough to make a man go mad!

Somewhere a switch was turned. One by one the great hanging chandeliers glowed into light, casting a yellow hue on the strained faces of the marshals so that they looked as if they had been greased with vaseline. Beria stopped his jokes. Suddenly he tugged at the jacket of his suit like some counter-jumper of a clerk going for an interview for a job at the GOUM**. Hastily the marshals did the same. The Dictator was going to speak!

Slowly, very slowly, Stalin took the curved working man's pipe which he affected out of his mouth. 'In my homeland, Georgia,' he said softly, his Georgian accent suddenly very pronounced, 'they used to say, "Out of shit, princes are made!"'

The marshals stared in bewilderment at their master sitting there on his throne. What were they supposed to do? Suddenly Beria laughed, high-pitched and feminine. Immediately these burly tough men, who commanded the destinies of millions, did the same in their gruff, bass soldier's way.

Stalin smiled faintly. Whether it was because he thought they appreciated the meaning of his statement or because

*The Russian Secret Police
**A Moscow store

they had reacted sycophantically, the marshals did not know or care. Here in the Kremlin it was always wiser to do as the rest did – and safer, too.

'From the shit of last autumn, that rabble which let the Fritzes capture them by the hundred thousand, those swine who ran almost back to Moscow itself, that scum which even *volunteered* to fight for the Fritzes,' Stalin's voice rose angrily and the marshals trembled (were heads going to roll?), 'we have at last created – *an army*!' Stalin's voice dropped – and he actually smiled again.

Collectively the marshals breathed an inner sigh of relief. He was not going to criticise their performance in 1941 when the Fritzes had caught them completely by surprise and whole Soviet armies had run away or surrendered.

'Now, Comrade Marshals,' Stalin continued, 'all evidence shows that the Fritzes are going to have another go.' He nodded to Beria.

Beria cleared his throat nervously and the marshals felt a little better. Beria was as frightened of his fellow-countryman as they all were. 'Our directors* and illegal residents throughout Western Europe indicate that the Fritzes are moving east again in strength,' he began. 'From northern France and the Belgian training areas our agents report that armoured formations are leaving daily for destinations unknown. A few of these formations are equipped with their latest tank, the Tiger, concerning which you comrades already know some of the details.'

The marshals, most of whom had been brought up with the horse in the Czarist cavalry, nodded their agreement hurriedly. All winter they had studied hard in their spare time, trying to understand the techniques of the Fritzes' armoured blitzkrieg which had burst through the Red Army the previous summer. More than the German soldier they feared the German superior employment of armour. Now the Fritzes were coming at them with their latest monster, all

*Heads of secret intelligence

sixty tons of it, and their own T-34 weighed half of that!

'What will be their objective this time?' Beria continued. 'Our information is that it is going to be to the south. The Fritzes will mark time on both the northern and central fronts.' He looked at Stalin.

In his turn Stalin looked at Marshal Timoshenko, the commander of all Soviet forces between the Rivers Donets and the Don, but said nothing.

The ex-sergeant, who now commanded five armies and a whole armada of armoured formations in the south, actually blushed, a sudden tic starting up on the left side of his face, the face of a determined, stubborn man. 'We strike first!' he managed to say, head twisted to one side as if his collar were too tight for him.

Old Leather Face nodded encouragingly.

'As I did in January, Comrade Secretary,' Timoshenko hurried on, 'but with more strength. Two pincers from Izyum and Volchansky: objective Kharkov, the administrative centre of the Ukrainian heavy industry. Hit them hard, hit them first!' he concluded.

Stalin allowed himself a faint smile, though his dark, unrevealing eyes did not light up. 'I see you are trying to teach me a little Russian geography, Comrade Marshal,' he said softly. '*Kharkov, the administrative centre of the Ukrainian heavy industry*, eh? How nice to know that.'

Beria tittered, hand held delicately in front of his false teeth; the marshals frowned and looked down at the toes of their highly polished boots, as if embarrassed.

Timoshenko began to stutter something, the sweat pouring down his broad peasant face in long rivulets, but Stalin stopped him with an upraised hand.

What seemed an eternity of silence followed. Again the only sound in that great, high-roofed hall was that of marching feet and the jingle of Moscow's trams. Now and then the sweating marshals dabbed their dripping brows surreptitiously with their handkerchiefs. Once more the tension was almost unbearable. Anger mixed with fear in the heart of Marshal Timoshenko. Old Leather Face was a sadistic swine; he always tortured his soldiers thus, though they were the ones who had saved him and his whole damned corrupt system the previous winter. One day . . . one day, he promised himself, but he knew that day of revenge would never come. The threat was an idle one, not worth wasting breath on. His fellow marshals would never support him. Here Stalin broke his soldiers, one by one, and the others simply stood by and watched until their turn came.

'In essence, Comrade Marshal,' Stalin suddenly broke that heavy brooding silence in a manner that made even the toughest of them start with surprise, 'I agree with your suggestion. Hit them hard, hit them first! It has a nice ring about it. *But*,' the Dictator raised a nicotine-stained forefinger in warning, 'can we achieve both those aims?' He answered his own question. 'We cannot. My information, Comrade Timoshenko, is that you will not be ready to launch your attack for another four weeks.'

Timoshenko flashed a look at Beria. The Chief of the Secret Police was smiling in a smug, self-satisfied manner. So that was it: the big marshal, Beria, had spies even in his senior headquarters. How else could Old Leather Face know the state of his readiness?

'So,' Stalin continued, 'somehow or other we must delay the Fritzes, put them off balance until we are ready to attack their Sixth Army. Now I will have no further piecemeal attacks, frittering away human resources to no great purpose. No, Comrade Timoshenko, you will hold on to your every formation so that you can strike the Fritzes in *overwhelming strength* in one month's time! So how are we going to delay them until we are ready?' Again he nodded to Beria.

Beria was right on cue. 'Partisans!' he snapped. 'On the whole, those damned Ukrainians have supported the Fritzes so far. The Fritzes have made them all sorts of promises about independence and that kind of claptrap after the war. So we can receive little support from that source. So where do we find large numbers of ready-made partisans to harass the

Fritzes and slow down their preparations on their Sixth Army's front? I shall tell you, comrades.'

Now, for the first time since the anxious marshals had trooped into that great hall to meet their master, they forgot their fear. Curiosity drove it away. Where in the name of the Black Virgin of Kazan was Beria going to find a partisan army to operate in the Ukraine, which was as notoriously pro-German as it had been in the Old War when they all had been sergeants with the Red Cavalry?

Beria smiled thinly, enjoying his moment of triumph. In his throne-like chair, Stalin frowned. Comrade Beria was getting too big for his boots. He would have to keep an eye on him. Very definitely!

'Come on, Comrade Beria,' he growled, 'let us have it. Where are you going to find your partisans?'

'*Horoscho*, Comrade Stalin . . . Immediately, Comrade Stalin!' Beria said hurriedly, knowing he had gone too far, but still proud of the surprise he was going to spring on them – including Old Leather Face. 'I am going to open the gates of the Gulag,' he announced.

There was a gasp of shock. Even Stalin's leather poker-face showed surprise at the enormity of Beria's proposal.

'*Da, da*. You heard me correctly, comrades, open the Gulag, that is what I am going to do. Now that scum we have been locking up for so long will have to learn this – they either march or croak. That's the way it will be from now on, *march or croak!*'

Now everywhere along the long line of Soviet concentration camps, the Gulag Archipelago, as it was called, the riders from Beria's HQ came clattering in to bring their tidings, tugging at the bits of their sweat-lathered mounts and shouting out their bold invitation to these ragged, half-starved wretches Beria had imprisoned: 'Listen you rats. Russia needs bodies, even such miserable bodies as yours. The Motherland is bleeding hard. The Fritzes are about to attack again and we need volunteers to make up our losses. Step forward any man who wishes to volunteer to fight for his beloved Motherland!'

But of course there was never a single volunteer. Why should these broken men volunteer to fight for a system which had imprisoned them for their political beliefs? Why should the scum of Soviet society, the pimps, the thieves, the murderers, risk their precious lives for Russia? Why should the Balts, the Letts, the Mongols and the multi-coloured representatives of a dozen minorities fight for a nation which had taken away their independence so brutally?

But back in Moscow Beria had already made his provisions for the lack of enthusiasm for the Soviet Union's cause among this last great reservoir of manpower. It was the old tactic of sugar and the whip. '*Paparoki . . . vodka . . !*' the recruiting officer would order. '*Kleba . . . masla . . . pivo . . .*' And suddenly the camp's storemen would be hurrying out with drink and food, the like of which these poor starving wretches in rags had never seen for years.

'*Cigarettes . . . vodka . . . bread . . . butter . . !*' They uttered each word broken-voiced and awed, hardly daring to believe the evidence of their own eyes. Suddenly all discipline broke. No longer were they afraid of the guards with their cruel knouts and rifles. They surged forward in a great howling mob, seized the food from the storemen's arms and devoured it in huge gulps, tears of joy streaming down their pinched, weathered faces.

A little later the machine-guns would be set up facing the now drunken mob, the greencaps'* faces set and hard as they squatted cross-legged behind their weapons, waiting for Beria's messenger's orders.

Now the messenger – and half a hundred like him throughout the Gulags that month – laid it on the line, face set in a look of utter contempt as the drunken mob fell silent, faces suddenly ashen with fear at the sight of the grim silent

*Nickname given to the Secret Police due to their green insignia

machine-gunners with their weapons trained upon them. 'All right, I know it's no use appealing to the patriotism of scum like you. You've had your fill. You've got some spirit in your guts now. So what is it going to be? Your freedom, cancellation of your sentence, the same rations as an honest soldier of the Red Army – *or this!*' He swept his arm out dramatically at the line of gunners. 'It only takes one order from me and you're all dead on the spot – and good riddance too!'

Minutes later they were fighting and clawing each other to line up to volunteer, swearing an oath on that red flag with its hammer and sickle insignia they all hated, for one reason or another, so passionately. Everywhere the 'volunteers' Timoshenko needed came flooding in in their hundreds, their thousands. The campaign to delay Paulus's great push could commence . . .

CHAPTER 2

THE SHABBY Russian frontier-town, knee-deep in mud and dirt, swarmed with life. As the long troop train braked to a stop, the population descended upon the gaping Wotan troopers, crying out in half a dozen languages. '*Brot!*' the ragged Ukrainian women and children in their sack-cloth aprons pleaded, making desperate gestures with their hands, as if they might well die on the spot if the Germans did not immediately start throwing them bread. Jews, still not rounded up and sent to the camps, dressed in rusty-black, their 'belly-shops' clasped to their skinny guts, tendered their wares. 'Schnaps for the German gentlemen!' they cried hopefully in Yiddish. 'Excellent one hundred per cent potato schnaps!' Cheeky little urchins with bright black eyes and gleaming curly hair, obviously gypsies, waved pictures at the gaping greenhorns and made obscene gestures with their fingers, proclaiming, 'Girls . . . beautiful girls for German soldiers . . . No pox, gentlemen . . . beautiful girls! *ficki-ficki gut . . .*'

A long line of prisoners in the earth-brown tunics of the Red Army plodded towards the marshalling yards, being driven through the crowd of civilians by middle-aged chaindogs mounted on *panje* ponies and wielding whips, who cried at intervals, '*Weg da, ihr Schweine . . . weg da . . . Jetzt kommen die Iwans . . .*'

The Vulture took his monocle out of his eye and cleaned it deliberately as the locomotive, with the usual slogan, '*Die Rader Rollen für den Sieg*',* painted on its bullet-pocked side, gave a grateful sigh as if it had a life of its own and came to a halt at the buffers. 'The New Order, as proclaimed by our beloved Führer Adolf Hitler, Captain von Dodenburg,' he

*Wheels Roll for Victory

announced, smugly. 'Pimps, panders and disgusting Popovs! The benefits of the One Thousand Year Reich* bestowed on these worthless wretches. How little they appreciate the boon of German *Kultur*, eh, my dear boy?'

Von Dodenburg took his eyes off a ragged gypsy boy who had slipped down his pants to expose his skinny naked rear to some gawping troops to make his offer all too clear. 'Some, *Obersturmbannführer*,' he replied, icily, 'might enjoy *those* fruits of German *Kultur*.' With a nod of his head he indicated the bending boy with his outrageous offer of sex.

The Vulture flushed angrily. 'Yes . . . yes,' he snapped. 'But let us not waste time. There are things to be done.'

Von Dodenburg nodded his agreement. Already he could see the pompous railway officials stamping up the platform, clip-boards at the ready, while *Luftwaffe* anti-aircraft gunners began rolling up their mobile 20mm flak cannons to protect the train, yet another of the many which crammed the marshalling yards, waiting for the cover of darkness before moving further into the Ukraine. 'Your orders sir?' he barked.

'The men will re-board the train at midnight, von Dodenburg. That will give them exactly six hours to debauch themselves in their usual piggish manner.'

Von Dodenburg indicated he understood. Nowadays at all these frontier crossings, before the men of the *Wehrmacht* went into the battles from which so few of them returned, they were allowed a last debauch. There were drinking dens and brothels everywhere, most of them supervised by the hated middle-aged 'rear-echelon stallions' of the Quartermaster's Branch.

'The men will, however, carry their weapons with them at all times, von Dodenburg,' the Vulture warned severely. 'I will not have my men attacked. Every man will be checked on his return to the train to see that he is still in possession of it. There will be no selling of weapons to the partisans in SS Assault Regiment Wotan! Is that clear, von Dodenburg?'

---

*Hitler maintained his empire would last a thousand years

'Yessir!' von Dodenburg replied, noting out of the corner of his eye that his CO was eyeing the half-naked gypsy boy with some interest now. He could guess where the Vulture would spend his last few hours before the Regiment departed for the front. 'Shall I ask the local quartermaster for an issue of Parisians* for the men, sir?'

The Vulture looked at the younger officer as if he were an idiot. 'God in heaven, von Dodenburg, do you really believe that it is still important to ensure the men don't get the pox? My dear boy, most of them will be long dead before this spring is out.' He grinned maliciously at von Dodenburg's sudden discomfiture and the latter realised he was being paid back for his reference to the half-naked boy.

'Rotten with syphilis or not, ...ose greenbeaks back there will have each died a hero's death for . . . er . . . *Folk, Fatherland and Führer.* That is all, Captain. Now, von Dodenburg, release them and let them get on with their wretched working-class piggeries. They have got exactly . . .'

Joyously the troopers, whooping like Red Indians, swarmed down from the train, released at last after five cramped, boring days and were absorbed at once into that mob of half a dozen nationalities. By now this mixture of Poles, Russians, Ukrainians, Gypsies and Jews had long lost their fear of the *nmetski*, even if they were the SS. For centuries they had lived under different masters, all as cruel and unpredictable as the Germans, and they had come to terms with that fact. One day, sooner or later, they would die, but till that time came they had to live – and to do that they had to offer a service: their wares, their bodies, their wives' bodies, their children's bodies. They had done it long before; they did it now, unthinkingly and without hate or rancour, just concerned that they received the highest possible price for what they had to give . . .

*Army slang for contraceptives

Some of the soldiers' tastes were easy. Schulze and Matz immediately joined the long queue outside the nearest NCO brothel, their money held eagerly in one hand, the log of wood which was part of the price for the whore's services (she needed the wood to heat her room) in the other. Most of the young officers had nothing else in their minds but to enjoy a huge meal of the first fresh food they had eaten in days, wolfing down great platefuls of *Bratkartoffeln*, Polish gherkins and fried eggs, faces flushed with good health, the grease running unheeded down their unshaven chins. But there were those who had special tastes. Sergeant-Major Metzger, 'the Butcher', was one of those. As he remarked to the captain quartermaster, a fat jolly fellow full of bonhomie and schnaps, known to all as 'Father Christmas' on account of his shock of snow-white hair, 'It's not that I have real problems with the old salami. But all the strain of this move, you know . . .' He twisted awkwardly, as if his collar were too tight for him. '. . . It has a certain effect on a feller's . . . er . . . outside plumbing.'

Father Christmas slapped him on the arm. 'I understand perfectly, Sergeant-Major . . . Say no more . . . As one man of the world to another, I know your problem. What is the old witticism? *Frustration* is the first time it won't go up for the second time. *Desperation* is the second time it won't go up the *first* time, what? Ha ha!'

'Yes, Father Christmas, something like that,' the Butcher agreed weakly. 'But you see them Polack whores of yours might not understand my . . . er little dilemma. I'd rather like to have a German lady, if you have one in stock.'

'Naturally, Sergeant-Major Metzger,' Father Christmas boomed happily. He made a swift counting gesture with his thumb and fat forefinger, both of which were none too clean, as befitted a quartermaster service notorious throughout the German Army for the bribes it took. 'For a small consideration, I think we can find you a suitable and very sympathetic *German* lady.'

Thus it was that the Butcher met Fräulein Schmitz, known

among Quartermaster circles as 'Juicy Lucy' on account of her fabled qualities in that nether region, and coincidentally became the harbinger of the bad news that all was not well with the coming offensive . . .

'Hm,' Juicy Lucy Schmitz said as she towered above Metzger on the bed, naked save for a pair of too-tight black kneeboots and her pince-nez, staring down at the Butcher's naked body critically. 'It ain't doing much, is it?' she opined.

Next door in the special quartermaster brothel, the bed springs were squeaking lustily and a German voice was gasping, *'For Chrissake, hold on to me heels, I think I'm gonna disappear into it . . .!'*

The Butcher stared up at the massive naked whore as an inexperienced alpinist might do as he eyed the peaks of Mount Everest for the first time. 'I've been under a lot of strain, Fräulein Schmitz,' he said meekly.

'I see,' she murmured, as if she were a doctor trying to assess the gravity of a patient's condition. She took a pencil from her bedside table and used it to lift the Butcher's flaccid organ. 'Has it been like this for a long time?' she asked.

Next door the unknown German was saying angrily now, *'Coming, yer say . . . You're coming like Christmas is frigging coming, miss . . . Next frigging year!'*

'A few weeks, er months,' the Butcher corrected himself hurriedly, noting the severe look behind Juicy Lucy Schmitz's pince-nez. 'Well, over six months now, ever since we came back from Greece in the summer of '41.'

'You didn't get a certain disease there, did you?' she asked severely. 'You know all those foreign women are poxed up to the eyes.'

'No, no, *Fräulein,*' he assured her hastily. 'I don't know . . . it just happened. Of course, I'm married. That might have had something to do with it. As you know, married women are at heart nuns. They don't like the old salami.'

Fräulein Juicy Lucy did not seem to hear his comments on married women. Instead she indicated the marks on his thighs with her pencil. 'You've had the treatment, I see. Did it help?'

Involuntarily the Butcher shuddered at the memory of that French woman, clad in funeral black, who had handed him the brush and then proffered her booted foot for him to polish, before picking up the whip and commanding harshly, 'Now clean, you German swine . . . Or by God, you'll regret the day you were born!'

'No, *Fräulein*, it only hurt. Oh, how it hurt!' he moaned.

She nodded her understanding. 'Never been fond of the treatment myself, I must confess. All right, Sergeant-Major.' She made her decision, as next door that German voice complained plaintively, 'What! For one hundred Reichsmark, *no afters* . . !* Don't you realise that I'm on my way to the frigging front to have my turnip blown off and you call yerself a frigging German patriot!'

'All you have to do is to relax. Think of nothing, just pleasure. In one moment I shall lower myself on your . . . er . . . thing, Sarn't-Major, and you will find out why they call me Juicy Lucy . . . If you listen to me and do exactly as I say, I can assure you here and now that your salami will be so stiff it'd knock a duchess's tea-cup off the table, if you ever had occasion to go to tea with a duchess!' She giggled girlishly and Sergeant-Major Metzger tensed and prepared to bear the strain as she spread her dimpled knees and began to lower her massive bulk upon that all-important 'salami'.

But it was not to be.

Suddenly, frighteningly, the voice of the unknown German next door, who would never receive his 'afters' despite the high-price he had paid to the whore, gasped, 'Hey, what are you Slavic shit-shovellers doing here? *Can't you see that an honest German male is trying to –*'

The rest of his words were drowned by the shrill scream of the whore and the dull boom of a hand grenade exploding. Suddenly the big bed trembled underneath an expectant Butcher, his eyes tightly screwed together as he readied himself to bear Juicy Lucy's weight. He opened his eyes swiftly. Juicy Lucy was still there, at least most of her enormous body was, except for her head. That was sailing through the air, pursued by the rest of the disintegrating wall, while a very wet underbody descended upon his reluctant salami and his naked chest became abruptly awash with bright-red blood. He opened his mouth to scream. To no avail! A big tit plumped down and blocked all sound.

Thus in death Juicy Lucy saved Sergeant-Major Metzger from the terrible fate that was to be suffered by the rest of those unfortunate visitors to the Quartermaster Corps special de luxe brothel . . .

Next door they were raping one of the whores. Out of the corner of his eye, a terrified Butcher could see what was going on through the great ragged hole in the wall. There were three of them, ragged and half-starved in appearance, but definitely very frightening, as they held the screaming whore down while a fourth prepared to mount her. 'No!' she shrieked, writhing back and forth, her big breasts flying all around. 'It is not allowed! I'm a German . . . Slavs are not allowed to touch me by law . . .' Her protests ended abuptly as the fourth man slit her throat and plunged his organ into her heaving, dying body in one and the same movement.

Desperately the Butcher sucked at Juicy Lucy's nipple like a baby at its mother's breast, waiting for his turn while all about him his fellow Germans died violently and suddenly.

It came – savagely. A drunken voice cried out loud and suddenly the door reeled open, its hinges shattered, as someone fired a burst with a machine-pistol through it. Desperately the terrified Butcher tried to make himself even smaller beneath the naked hulk of dead, headless flesh. '*Yo tuoyo matr!*' someone cursed grossly in Russian and then for some reason added in slurred German, '*tot* . . . both dead . . !'

Metzger caught himself from sighing in sheer relief just at the last second. They thought he was dead too. He waited until the sound of the heavy boots disappeared down the corridor and then, cautiously, very cautiously, he peered out from beneath the dead whore.

He gasped with shock. Not all the ragged, savage invaders had gone. Swaying drunkenly at the shattered door, there was a little slant-eyed fellow who looked like some kind of Chink, with a wooden leg and a very large knife, its blade gleaming with fresh blood, in his hand. But the Chink had other things than murder on his mind now. His black eyes sparkled excitedly as they gazed at Juicy Lucy's monstrous naked rump and already he was fumbling excitedly with his flies. The Butcher's heart nearly stopped beating with horror. Once the Chink mounted the whore, drunk or not, he'd soon discover him there, and that damned sabre of the Chink's looked very, very frightening. Coward that he was, Sergeant-Major Metzger knew he would have to act, and act fast.

In the very same instant that the would be rapist managed to undo his flies and was poised there drunkenly, swaying slightly as he prepared to lunge, the Butcher flung dead Juicy Lucy to one side, kicked the Chink's wooden leg from beneath him and threw his whole massive naked bulk onto the totally surprised rapist. He went out like a light. Sergeant-Major Metzger had his prisoner . . .

Sweating furiously in spite of the biting cold, the Vulture snapped off shots to left and right as the handful of greenbeaks under von Dodenburg tried desperately to set up the machine-gun on the roof of the train. Their attackers were everywhere. Now they were swarming out of the burning township, running heavily through the mud towards the marshalling yards, obviously intent on looting and wrecking the troop trains grouped there. 'In three devils' name!' the Vulture bellowed above the snap and crack of small arms fire, 'get that MG working! They'll be among the Tigers in half a moment!' He ripped off an angry burst and a giant of a Russian went reeling back, his chest a scarlet, shattered mess, his arms flailing the air as if he were climbing the rungs of an invisible ladder.

His heart beating like a furious trip-hammer, von

Dodenburg, fully aware of the emergency, thrust the greenbeak away from the MG 42. 'Load,' he yelled desperately. 'For Chrissake, *load*!' He flung himself behind the long-barrelled machine gun while the loader fed in the long belt of gleaming bullets, his clumsy fingers numb with cold.

Now their attackers were scrambling over the top of the next troop train, dropping grenades down the barrels of the cannon on the flat cars, spraying gasoline on the wagons from open cans and igniting it with a great *whoosh*. In half a minute they'd be finished with the already burning train and attacking Wotan's long line of flat cars and carriages.

The sweating, red-faced loader slapped him on the shoulder. '*IN*!' he yelled. The belt was loaded.

Von Dodenburg waited no longer. He pressed the trigger. The MG 42 burst into high-pitched, hysterical life. Frantically von Dodenburg swung the gun from left to right. Like lethal bees, the tracer bullets raced towards the attackers.

'*Ai-i-i!*' That terrible scream seemed to go on for ever as the first frenetic burst ripped into a bunch of drunken Russians grouped around the next train's locomotive. They were galvanized into a crazy dance, arms and legs twitching maniacally, as that deadly burst smacked into their bodies at such close range. In an instant they were thrown, writhing and twitching, into the mud like a group of bloody, broken dolls.

Von Dodenburg swung the gun to the left. Face tense and hard, gleaming with sweat as if greased with vaseline, he fired a long burst at a group of attackers attempting to set up one of those old-fashioned Soviet machine-guns complete with little shield.

They went down in a sudden heap, choking on their own blood, their faces pulped a bright scarlet. The Russian number two attempted to rise. Von Dodenburg didn't give him a chance. 'Die pig . . . *die!*' he cried fervently, carried away by the atavistic lust of battle, and pressed the trigger again. The number two went down, screaming with agony, his intestines pouring out of his ruptured belly onto the cold

mud. Frantically he attempted to put them back with
bloodied claws. To no avail. They slipped through his wet
fingers and dropped to the ground, hot, steaming, obscene.

Now the troopers of SS Wotan were returning the enemy's
fire everywhere. Schulze and Matz came running from the
shattered brothel, in their hands a chamber pot full of
grenades which they began lobbing to left and right like
lethal Easter eggs. Russians went down on all sides. A huge
brute of a Russian attempted to grab Schulze's leg, as he lay
there dying in the mud.

Schulze didn't hesitate. He launched a tremendous kick at
the Russian with his cruelly nailed dice-beaker. 'Croak,
Popov, *croak!*' he cried as the Russian fell back screaming, his
stainless steel teeth bulging out of his mouth. Behind Schulze,
Matz slammed his foot into them and ground them deep into
the mud. 'Fuckin' well eat shit – *Ivan!*' he cried mercilessly,
and ran on, lobbing his grenades to left and right with gay
abandon.

The steam started to go out of the surprise attack. On all
sides, the Russians were meeting resistance. Slowly but surely
they began to fall back, burning and slaughtering as they did
so, leaving ever more still shapes behind in the mud as they
retreated out of the marshalling yards into the merrily
burning frontier town. Von Dodenburg and the men of
Wotan, perched on the train's roof, followed them with a
cruel barrage, waiting for the Russians to be illuminated a
stark black against the blazing scarlet flames of the petrol fires
before they opened up, the angry tracer bullets zipping
through the glowing gloom and stitching a frightening
pattern at their flying heels.

Below in the cover of the armoured cab of the locomotive
with its bold legend, the Vulture nodded his approval. Let
the other fools of the infantry regiments venture forth to
attack the retreating Popovs and have their stupid turnips
blown off. His men, veterans and greenbeaks, were conserving
their strength, retaining their positions without risk. He
wanted SS Assault Regiment Wotan intact for the start of the

great offensive which would surely bring him his full general's stars.

Suddenly the Vulture gasped. A huge man, clasping a strange-looking bundle under his arm and naked save for his dice-beakers and helmet, was running across the body-littered marshalling yard, zig-zagging crazily, going all-out as if the Devil himself were after him. 'Heaven, arse and cloudburst!' he choked as a sudden grenade illuminated the running figure in a burst of glowing incandescent white. '*It's Sergeant-Major Metzger!*'

The Butcher it was, and now ensconced on the roof of the train next to von Dodenburg, Schulze chortled, 'Willya get a load of that, sir. It's the Butcher, bringing a present for the lads . . . Holy strawsack, it's a frigging Popov . . . Hope we don't have to eat the frigger . . .'

But that alarming possibility would not be realised. Pegleg Izzy, as the little Jew whom the Butcher had captured in such a strange manner in the Quartermaster brothel that wild night was named, would prove to be too valuable a prisoner for that . . .

CHAPTER 3

'THERE'LL BE a piece of nice tin in this for you, Metzger,' the Vulture announced as he surveyed their prisoner, now calmly eating a sausage sandwich which one of the kitchen bulls had specially prepared for him.

The Butcher beamed and Pegleg Izzy nodded his approval, his cunning black Jewish eyes missing nothing, as the long troop train set off once again, leaving the burning border city behind it. All his wretched life as a peddler of knicker-elastic to Russian peasant women, who only wore knickers on special occasions as it was, he had been waiting for something like this: to be the centre of attraction of a group of high-ranking officers who were both foreign and important. Weren't some of them even aristocratic, to judge by the names that were being passed back and forth? He puffed out his skinny chest proudly. His decision to 'volunteer' for the partisans had been the right one after all. Through it he had found new friends, *goyim* though they might be, who respected the former knicker-elastic salesman, as he had never been respected before. He curbed his desire to take a large bite of the excellent German sausage, not because he half-suspected it was not quite *kosher*, but because he did not want his new-found friends to think him wanting in social graces, and announced in his queer mixture of Yiddish and what he considered German, 'They had a plan, you see, gentlemen. They thought they'd flood the front with the people of the Gulag to deflect the impact of our German attack.'

The Vulture looked at him and then at von Dodenburg, as the long, heavy troop train began to gather speed, and laughed, 'Our German attack, eh, von Dodenburg? He'll be asking to join the SS soon, *our* little Yiddish friend will.'

Hurriedly the little prisoner shook his head. He was not *that* enamoured of his new friends. 'Gladly, gentlemen,' he exclaimed winningly, his hands fluttering back and forth like caged birds, 'gladly would I sacrifice my life for our noble cause. But my leg . . .' He tapped the wooden leg with his knuckles like a smart dealer testing the quality of a piece of antique furniture. . . . 'It would not allow me to do so.'

'Ask our tame Yid whether he thinks there are many more of these Gulag wretches roaming around, von Dodenburg?' the Vulture commanded. 'I have a feeling that our troop trains to the front are going to come in for special attention from these rats.'

But Pegleg Izzy did not need von Dodenburg's question to send him off again into a voluble explanation. 'Of course, *Herr General*,' he said hastily, putting down his sandwich and looking at the Vulture 'Of course! Those Russian swine want to stop our gallant boys from getting to the front.'

Von Dodenburg grinned at 'our gallant boys' and told himself that the little Jew was a card. 'And then what, Jew?'

The former knicker-elastic salesman shrugged elegantly, as if it were the most obvious thing in the world. 'Am I *meschugge*? Do I have little birds that go *tweet-tweet* in my belfry? Have I got air in my teeth? *Then what?* Ain't it obvious, *Herr General?*' He addressed the Vulture directly. 'Then they attack our own brave German boys . . . that's what, gentlemen.' Almost as if to emphasize his point, a burst of machine-gun fire ripped the length of the officers' compartment, making them all duck instinctively, all except the little Jew, who waved his hand cheerfully and said, 'You see what I mean, gentlemen. Those Gulag rats are everywhere!' So saying, he picked up his sausage sandwich once more and dug into it heartily, a happy and, in his eyes, a respected man . . .

Those same sentiments animated Sergeant Schulze a few compartments away as he squatted in front of the stove, occupying the Butcher's usual place in his absence, daintily digging the dirt out from underneath his toenails and holding

forth for the benefit of the younger NCOs among the crowd.
Waving the bayonet he was using for the operation, he said,
'Now you bunch of wet-tails are gonna be in for some
surprises up there, once we hit the spot where the shit flies.
There's the flies for one thing. They've got Popov mosquitoes
up there that can blow yer kisser up to the size of a football
with one bite. And the bees,* Christ the bees! Many's the
time I've counted hundreds of the little shits in the seams of
my shirt alone.' He pointed his bayonet at a young lance-
corporal who was already beginning to scratch as if he were
ridden with lice. 'And remember this, the bees multiply
twelve times daily. That's all they do – *fuck and feed off us
humans!*' He dug the tip of the bayonet in and neatly excised a
piece of stubborn dirt from beneath his big toe-nail. It flew
into the eye of the scratching lance-corporal. Schulze did not
appear to notice, however.

'Yes,' Matz took up the theme, 'the way them Popov bees
multiply, if you don't do a little bit of daily pest control, you
could have thousands of the friggers running all over yer in a
week or so. Why, the first time we went out and I didn't take
proper care, I found a whole bunch of the little buggers right
under my foreskin.' He laughed crazily. 'Think what that
could have done to my sex life!'

The lance-corporal turned very pale and gagged dramatically, as if he might begin vomiting at any moment.

'Then there's the rats. Up there at the front, they can grow
to the size of a small pony!' Schulze declared, taking up the
recital once more. 'It's on account of all the stiffs lying all over
the place. More than once I've seen the buggers carry off the
company cat and eat it there and then! Yessir, they say that
Reichsführer SS Himmler had ordered a special breed of
roof-hare**to be developed in Berlin to cope with them
Russian rats!' He dug his bayonet into a particularly
stubborn piece of dirt and wrenched hard. 'Yes, you

*Army slang for 'lice'
**Army slang for 'cat'

greenbeaks are gonna have the shock of yer young lives once we hit the front.'

'And you, Sergeant Schulze, are going to have a shock – *right now!*' the Butcher's well-known voice boomed into the happy little group, crowded round the stove.

Schulze didn't look up. He pretended to concentrate on the dirt, saying innocently, 'Did somebody just fart?'

But the Butcher was in too good a humour to be offended by Sergeant Schulze's remark. He pushed into the packed compartment, followed by his new 'friend' Pegleg Izzy, who had ensured, after all, that he would receive 'a nice piece of tin', and barked, as the greenbeaks sprang awkwardly to attention, 'Didn't you hear that burst of MG fire just now, Schulze?'

'Thought it was them greenbeaks loosing off their fart-cannons, Sar'nt-Major,' Schulze replied, putting on his boots, his 'ablutions', as he called them, finished for this night. 'We had pea soup for supper, you may remember.'

'I don't!' the Butcher snapped. 'But no matter. According to the Vulture and this here little Yiddish Jew' – he indicated Izzy with a jerk of his thumb and the little former knicker-elastic salesman bowed grandly – 'we might well be in for some trouble. He's already ordered that the gunners get out and man the MGs of their Tigers. Now he wants somebody up front with a MG 42 to protect the locomotive, and that somebody is going to be *you*, Sergeant Schulze, and that perverted little banana-sucker friend of yours, Corporal Matz.' He ended with a malicious grin. 'Now get yer fart-cannon out of my place! Me and my friend want to warm ourselves.'

'But why us?' Matz protested. 'Why can't these greenbeaks do it? They're keen as mustard, *aren't yer?*' Matz dug his skinny elbow viciously into the young lance-corporal and the latter gasped hurriedly, 'Oh yes, Sergeant-Major, I'll volunteer for one, sir.'

'Fuck off, wet-tail!' the Butcher barked in his usual gallant manner. 'I want a couple of veterans like you two up front.

Then I know I can lay my little head down safely to sleep, with you two protecting me. Now no more chat. Get the popgun and – *pop off* . . !

Thus it was, while the Butcher and Pegleg Izzy occupied the straw in front of the pot-bellied stove, already well warmed by Sergeant Schulze and Corporal Matz, the two friends were forced out into the cruel night to take up their post with the MG 42 on top of the tender, searching the darkness for the elusive enemy.

Behind them in the crowded compartments, those not on duty began to settle down for the night. *'Gute Nacht, Kameraden'* came from all sides. Here and there troopers thrust home a last log into the glowing stoves and settled down with their back to the warmth, ignoring the first stirrings of the new lice. They were the veterans. They had seen it all before; they knew what to expect, including the lice.

But there were many that night, as the train pounded ever closer to their date with destiny, who could not sleep. Listening to the monotonous roll and beat of the train's steel wheels, they were lost in dreams of another life, their gazes trying to penetrate the red-glowing gloom of the crowded carriages, minds full of sombre shadows and dark forebodings. They were on their way to the front. That they knew. But what horrors lay ahead of them in the ghost-ridden wastes of this enormous, hostile country? What horrors indeed . . .?

Schulze awoke from his doze with a start. Grumpily he brushed away the icicle which had begun to form at the end of his big nose. Next to him on the heap of logs, Matz snored on, bowed over the MG 42. Schulze blinked his eyes several times, until finally everything came into focus.

It was already dawn and the long troop train was chugging desperately up a long extended incline. Below in the cab, the fireman tossed logs into the gaping, fiery maws of the boiler, trying to keep up the steam, while the driver moved from side to side nervously to peer up the slope.

Schulze knew why. On both sides the pass narrowed steadily between heights lined with snow-heavy firs. It would be an ideal site for an ambush. He nudged Matz. 'Hey, wake up, plush-ears!' he growled.

'Piss in the wind!' Matz muttered, steadfastly keeping his eyes screwed tightly shut. 'Zarah Leander* is just going to take off her black step-ins and show me *it*.'

'I'll show yer the back of me hand in a minute, if you don't have them glassy orbs open, Matzi!' Schulze threatened, doubling a fist like a small steam-shovel. 'We might be in for a little trouble here.'

Captain von Dodenburg thought the same. He rubbed his hand across the little square of steamed-up glass next to his seat and stared out at that barren, lonely countryside. It seemed to breathe hostility, though it appeared to be completely deserted. Yet already he had spotted the foot-prints in the snow leading up to the heights, with the firs marching across them like a battalion of spike-helmeted Prussian guards. 'What an ideal site for an ambush,' he whispered to himself, as the speed of the troop train rapidly diminished. Soon anyone on foot would be able to overtake them at this pace. He sat up suddenly and stared at the sleep-drunk, flushed faces all around him. If he was right and there was an ambush planned up there, how would the Popovs or these Gulag rats or whatever they were do it?

The fire-power of the flat cars, where the poor freezing gunners now manned the turrets of the Tigers, was immense. No one would be able to stop them. But what use would they be if the Popovs derailed the engine? In the final analysis the Vulture could order the Tigers unloaded, their decks packed with the panzer grenadiers, and they could continue under their own steam until they reached the nearest German military outpost.

The Vulture, seated opposite, seemed to share von Dodenburg's opinion, for opening his eyes and taking in the

*Famous German film star of the time

situation in his usual swift Regular Army manner, he snapped, 'No real cause for worry, von Dodenburg. Mind you, the train driver's piles won't be helped much if the mine goes off right under his locomotive, what! Ha ha!'

Von Dodenburg didn't smile. The Vulture's malicious kind of humour did not appeal to him. Instead he stood up with difficulty, buckled on his pistol belt, and grabbed his hat. 'All the same, sir, better have a look up front.'

The Vulture nodded his agreement. 'As you wish, von Dodenburg. And while you're up there, tell those lazy swine of kitchen bulls to put a good shot of vodka in my morning nigger-sweat. It's damnably cold in here!' He shivered dramatically.

But this particular March morning Colonel Geier was not fated to receive his coffee laced with vodka, or anything else for that matter.

In the very same moment that von Dodenburg moved to the door, there was a tremendous explosion to the rear. Frantically he grabbed for support as the carriage heaved and trembled and his nostrils were assailed by the acrid stench of burnt explosive. He gasped with shock. Instinctively he opened his mouth to prevent his eardrums from being burst.

Slowly but surely the train started to come to a halt while up front, crouched on the tender, Schulze and Matz gawped, open-mouthed as the flat cars containing the Tigers began to roll backwards down the long slope, detached from the body of the troop train by that cunningly placed mine. Pegleg Izzy gasped, striking his right cheek in admiration with his skinny little fist. 'Oy, oy, how smart . . . Dey must be Yiddish, dem bastards! . . . *Veh, oh veh*, de General ain't gonna like this, not one bit he is . . .'

Miserably watching the Tigers, manned only by the single gunners locked in each turret, disappear down the bend, the Vulture very definitely did not like it one bit . . .

CHAPTER 4

THE NEW snow foamed and whirled through the half-veiled trees, slashed across the hillside and was urged to new fury by every gust of the frenzied, shrieking wind. But even the snowstorm could not deaden the *thump thump* of gunfire on the other side of the hill where the flat cars lay stranded. It was obvious that a full-scale battle was going on down there and the greenbeaks, without NCOs and officers, were putting up a good show for themselves. The question now was how long they could hold out?

Von Dodenburg held up his hand. Behind him the little assault group of NCOs came to a ragged halt, the snowflakes pounding their crimson faces, working their way into nostrils, ears and eyes, poking into them with icy, numbing fingers. But the veterans did not seem to notice. Their whole attention was concentrated on the trapped flat cars. They too knew that time was running out. The Russians would soon change their tactics and begin assaulting the lone gunners one by one, and then they would be finished.

Von Dodenburg glanced at his watch. There was a minute to go. 'All right,' he choked, 'this is the plan. The other group under the CO will put in the feint attack in sixty seconds over there on the right flank. They'll make a lot of noise, but that will be about it. It'll be up to us to hit the Ivans hard and quick on the left flank. With a bit of luck we'll take them by surprise and roll them right up. Any questions?'

'Yessir.' As usual it was Sergeant Schulze, stick grenades stuck down his boots, MG 42, perched on his shoulder as if it were a child's toy.

'Fire away, you big rogue.'

'Can I apply for an immediate transfer to the Quartermaster Branch? I don't think I like this kind of soldiering, sir.'

Von Dodenburg grinned in spite of his inner tension. You

could always rely on Schulze to attempt to defuse a tight situation.

Across the valley there was the sudden *burr* of a machine-gun. Angry shouts drifted across to them. Von Dodenburg flung a glance in that direction. Tiny black figures were silhouetted against the white, stumbling forward in a ragged line. The Vulture's feint was going in, dead on time. '*Los!*' he cried, waiting no longer, '*Mir nach!*'

Hurriedly his NCOs spread out in attack formation, each man unslinging his weapon ready for the fight to come. At a half-double they slogged their way through the snow-heavy trees. On the other side of the valley they could hear the slower chatter of a Russian machine-gun, sounding like an angry woodpecker. The Popovs had engaged the Vulture's force, von Dodenburg told himself, hand gripping his pistol more tightly.

They breasted the hill and paused there momentarily to gain their breaths. Down below, the gunners in the Tigers were scything their immediate front with tracer, while the Gulag rats, dug into hollows of snow, returned their fire, little groups of them obviously trying to work closer, trying to get into the dead ground where the German fire could not reach them. In between the gunners and the Russians, the snow was littered with bodies; the greenhorns had made the enemy pay the price for their boldness.

'*Sturmangriff!*' von Dodenburg commanded.

They charged forward at once, all caution thrown to the winds now. Here and there the Russians turned in alarm and started firing wildly. Schulze cursed madly. Holding the heavy machine-gun tightly to his hip as if it weighed nothing, he ripped off a burst. Russians went down everywhere. They reached a dugout. Von Dodenburg yanked the pin out of a stick grenade and flung it into the darkness. It exploded in a furious burst of white smoke and yellow flame. A screaming Russian came staggering out, two scarlet pits where his eyes had been. Schulze let him have a burst in the chest. He rose high into the air under the impact of so much lead at such close range and landed in one of the trees, already dead, hanging there like some monstrous human fruit. They ran on . . .

But now the Russian resistance was thickening. In the turrets of the tanks, the gunners had ceased firing for fear of hitting their own men. The Russians dug in opposite seized the opportunity offered them and turned to face the advancing Germans. Now scarlet flame stabbed the white whirling gloom everywhere. The men of Wotan started to take casualties. Matz howled as a slug slammed into his upper arm and dropped to his right knee. Next to him another NCO fell screaming to the ground, his stomach ripped apart. With his free hand, Schulze tugged his running-mate to his feet. 'No fuckin' about now,' he gasped,' pretending yer fuckin' wounded!'

'What the shit do you think this is?' Matz yelled above the racket pointing to the blood dripping down his sleeve onto his hand. 'Frigging red paint?'

But Schulze had no time for answers. Instead he ripped off a quick burst at the gunner who had fired at Matz and the other man now writhing in the snow, fighting, or so it seemed, with the monstrous snake of his own guts.

Up front von Dodenburg shook his head. A ricochet had howled off his helmet. For a long moment he stood there in a complete daze. He shook his head hard. Everything came back into perspective. The Russians were getting out of their holes. They could see that the steam was going out of the German attack. In a few minutes they would rally sufficiently to charge themselves. 'Up here – Schulze!' he yelled urgently. '*At the double now!*'

'*Urrah!*' The hoarse bass cry rose from the Gulag Rats. They were coming!

Schulze and Matz flung themselves into the snow at the side of a kneeling Captain von Dodenburg. 'Salt 'em!' he commanded hurriedly. 'Salt the Popov shits . . . *quick!*'

Schulze needed no urging. The Russians were only a hundred metres away now, a ragged line of two hundred men or more, their bayonets held clutched to their sides, triumph written on their bearded, ratlike faces. In a moment they would swamp the pathetic little German line and that would be that. 'Hold on to yer frigging hat!' Schulze yelled exuberantly and pressed the trigger.

At 1000 rounds a minute, the MG 42 spat vicious fire. Expertly Schulze swung his gun from left to right, hosing the ranks of the cheering Russians.

They went down like ninepins. Still the survivors came on, animated by some desperate, wild courage. Frantically Schulze fired on, cursing furiously as the wounded Matz fed another belt into the air-cooled gun. At their side, von Dodenburg fired to left and right. Stumbling over the ranks of their own dead, the Russians charged. *Would nothing stop them?*

Suddenly the MG42 stopped! Von Dodenburg cursed. Next to him, Schulze shrieked something at a desperate Matz.

The Russians gave a wild yell of triumph. They redoubled their efforts, running awkwardly through the deep snow. Nothing could stop them now. They were only fifty metres away.

Schulze fumbled furiously at the breech of the machine-gun with fingers that felt like brittle icicles. Next to him, Matz ripped out the long belt of cartridges and started to thrust in another, crying obscenely to himself.

Von Dodenburg fired the rest of his magazine. The Russians went down on all sides, but they kept coming on. The situation was desperate. They'd be overrun in a minute. '*Grenades out!*' he yelled frantically.

Now he could make out the individual faces of the charging Russians, their features flushed with anger and aggression. In one second they would make their final rush – and it would be all over. Now they would show no mercy. They would slaughter the handful of Wotan troopers.

'Come on . . . come on . . . *come on, willya!*' Schulze shrieked. 'Get that fuckin' new magazine in . . . Matz, arse with ears, frigging well move it!'

'*IN!* Matz cried hysterically, eyes wide and wild with terror.

Schulze pressed the trigger, his chest heaving as if he had just run a great race. The Russians were only twenty metres away now. Abruptly the machine-gun erupted into vicious action. Purple flame stabbed the white air. Screaming obscenely, mad with fear and rage, Schulze traversed from left to right, scything his front with sudden, startling death.

In an instant the charging Russians seemed to disappear. One minute they were running, living men; the next they were dead or dying wretches, writhing and tossing in the snow, their faces contorted crazily by an unbearable agony.

Von Dodenburg hit Schulze on the shoulder. 'Cease fire!' he cried. 'Cease fire. . . conserve your ammo . . . *They've gone!*'

As if to signal that the Russians knew that their attack had failed a mortar bomb howled into the sky, to fall with an obscene thud. A blinding flash. A burst of bright white light. Fist-sized shards of silver-gleaming metal flew everywhere. Von Dodenburg ducked hastily. Gravel and snow showered his helmet. Five metres away a sergeant stared unbelievingly at the ragged gore of his stump as the blood jetted from his arm in a bright-red arc. Suddenly he fell face forward into the snow, his last dying scream muffled by the white waste.

Glumly, von Dodenburg waved his hand to left and right, the signal to dig in. Not only had the Russian counter-attack failed, but their own had too. The time had come to dig themselves deep into the frozen earth before the Popovs really started shelling them. Miserably the survivors took out their shovels and began to do so. Above them the lethal black eggs came raining down . . .

Like grey timber wolves, the three of them sneaked through the trees, the snowstorm howling around them, deadening any sound they might make. Behind them the rest of the NCO assault group fired at regular intervals to make the Russians believe the Germans were bogged down completely.

Von Dodenburg indicated wordlessly the first Russian dugout. Schulze nodded his understanding. For such a big man, he moved uncannily quietly, slipping on his 'Reeperbahn* Equaliser' as he did so. At the very last moment the Russian in the hole looked up. Too late. Schulze's cruel brass knuckles lashed out. The Russian went down as if poleaxed, spitting out teeth and blood as he did so.

Von Dodenburg signalled they should go on. Now they could see the squat, snow-shrouded shapes of the Tigers tied to the flat cars. Occasionally one of the trapped gunners would fire off a short burst, but mostly they were silent. Ammunition was in short supply; the gunners were conserving it for when the next Russian attack came, which would be soon. Von Dodenburg told himself the Russians would use the cover of the whirling snow storm too, now that they felt safe from a surprise attack from the rear.

Crouched now, the three of them advanced cautiously towards the last of the great tanks, knowing that everything depended upon the next few minutes. 'Sir!' Matz whispered urgently.

'What is it?' von Dodenburg hissed.

'Three o'clock, sir . . . Looks like an Ivan post . . . Big one too. Perhaps a command post.'

Von Dodenburg narrowed his eyes against the howling storm, not noticing the stinging snow with the tension. Matz was right. There was a Russian post there and it blocked all further progress. 'We take it out!' he commanded. 'Matz, as soon as you reach the flat car, get the gunner firing and start working on the chains. Off you go!'

Matz nodded his understanding and was off, his skinny little figure shrouded in snow almost immediately.

Von Dodenburg clasped his pistol more firmly in his hand. 'In and out – quick!' he ordered.

*The tough red-light district of Hamburg

'Like shit through a goose, sir!' Schulze agreed heartily.

Together they moved forward towards the unsuspecting Russians, their nostrils already assailed by their typical stink of sweat, boiled white cabbage and black tobacco. Now the command post was only ten metres away. Von Dodenburg knew their luck wouldn't hold much longer. 'All right, Schulze,' he commanded. '*NOW!*'

They sprang forward as one. A man with a beard leapt up from the hole, fumbling with a round-barrelled tommy gun. Schulze didn't give him a chance. His foot lashed out. The Russian reeled back screaming. Another Russian pushed him aside, sawing at the air with a sabre. Von Dodenburg pressed the trigger of his automatic. At that range he could not miss. The Russian's face seemed to disintegrate, his features slipping down to his chest like red molten wax.

Suddenly it was over. The remaining two Russians were throwing up their hands in absolute terror, yelling the only word of German they knew: '*Kamerad . . . Kamerad . . .*'

'Fuck off!' Schulze cried joyously and aimed a tremendous kick at the bottom of the taller of the two. That set them off and immediately the two Wotan men were doubling heavily through the snow towards the last tank, its machine-gun already blazing fire above their heads . . .

Furiously the three of them worked at the frozen chains which kept the Tiger anchored to the flat car, while slugs cut the air all around them as the enraged Russians prepared to attack yet again, some of them already crawling towards the dead ground which the gunners couldn't reach. With battered, bleeding hands they tore at the stiff chains, nerves jingling electrically with tension, hearts beating like crazy trip-hammers, knowing that time was running out rapidly.

The first Russian loomed out of the whirling white mist, long bayonetted rifle at the ready. Matz lashed out with his cruelly booted foot and the Russian disappeared howling back into the snowstorm. The other two didn't even look up. They had to get the damned chains loose or else . . .

Schulze, his face crimson with strain and rage, heaved his

brutally muscled shoulders and grunted. 'Move, you shit-thing, *move!*'

Suddenly the chain gave. A moment later von Dodenburg's did too. He wiped the sweat dripping from his brow away and yelled, 'Matz, into the driver's seat, we'll see to the rest –' He grabbed his pistol from the deck and fired instinctively. The Russian reeled back, clutching his hands tightly to his chest, through which blood escaped in a bright-red jet.

Von Dodenburg dropped his pistol again and concentrated on the remaining chains, while Matz, in spite of his wounded shoulder, jumped nimbly into the driver's compartment.

Now as they worked desperately to free the tank of its last restraints, they could hear the little corporal working at the engine. Madly von Dodenburg prayed it would start. In this terrible climate, he knew just how difficult it was to start motors not equipped with the special arctic-weather lubricating oils the Russians used. Slowly the dirge-like noise of the engine rose and rose. Yet stubbornly the motor refused to start. And the Russians were beginning to press home their attack. More and more of them were edging their way forward out of the dead ground.

'Done it!' Schulze yelled, rising.

'Done it too!' von Dodenburg cried the very next moment and sprang towards the tank. A Russian came running down the side of the flat car, machine-pistol blazing fire. The slugs howled off the metal just above von Dodenburg's head.

'Piss off!' Schulze cried. 'You can't do that to my officer, Popov prick!' He ripped the last of his stick grenades from the side of his jackboot, tugged the china pin and lobbed it straight at the running Russian. He ducked. The Russian didn't. He disappeared in a burst of evil purple flame.

Now the two of them clambered up onto the turret, where the teenage gunner, his face pale and tense with the strain of the long, lone battle, looked at them with doglike devotion, as if he might burst down and begin sobbing at any moment. Von Dodenburg clapped him on the shoulder. 'Well done,' he cried. 'Now batten down the hatches. We're in for trouble!'

'And you're not shitting kidding, sir!' Schulze agreed as they lowered the heavy steel hatch-cover. Already a furious, cursing Matz below in the driver's compartment was pumping the last of his special mix in a desperate attempt to start the obstinate motor, while the first of the Russians were beginning to swarm onto the flat car. In a moment they'd be attempting to dig their way into the tank.

Von Dodenburg grabbed the hand-crank which rotated the ten-ton turret. He could hear the first Russians clambering onto the Tiger's deck. Soon they'd begin attempting to lower grenades down the gun barrel or open the engine hatches. 'Here we go, Schulze!' he cried and began cranking.

Noisily the turret craned round. A shout of surprise. A bang. Someone cursed in Russian and fell to the ground. Schulze laughed. But the laugh died on his face almost immediately, as the turret started to flood with smoke and the freezing cold began to vanish rapidly, the stink of gasoline all too obvious. 'Shit on the shingle, sir!' he gasped. 'They're setting the frigging turret on fire!'

'They want to smoke us out!' von Dodenburg yelled, as down below Matz worked desperately on the reluctant engine. He choked and let go of the cranking handle.

Next to him the young gunner stared at Schulze, eyes wild and wide with fear, as the fumes, thick and choking, penetrated ever more rapidly into the turret. 'What can we do, Sarge?' he gasped.

'Frigging well pray!' Schulze yelled back and, wiping the sudden sweat from his brow, he cried down to Matz in his compartment, 'Hurry up and start the whoreson, Matz. Otherwise the Popovs'll be toasting yer eggs in double-quick time.'

Matz didn't even look up.

Another jerrican of fuel was splashed against the side of the burning turret. Von Dodenburg gasped for air. Next to him the young gunner broke down and started to sob. 'We'll be burned alive . . . Oh, mother, save me . . . *Mother, save me!*'

'Fuck yer mother!' Schulze cried crudely and slapped the boy hard.

The paint inside the turret was beginning to bubble and pop with the heat. In a moment, von Dodenburg knew, they would have to throw open the turret; they wouldn't be able to stand that tremendous heat. Already breathing was terribly difficult. Then the miracle happened. Perhaps the heat did it. With a sudden tremendous roar, the 400 HP engine burst into mighty, pulsating life.

Matz didn't wait for a command from von Dodenburg. He thrust home the first of the Tiger's thirty-odd gears and let out the clutch. The sixty-ton tank rumbled forward. '*Hold tight!*' an exuberant Matz cried.

Next moment the Tiger slammed to the ground with an earth-shaking thud. A moment later it was rumbling forward, its machine-gun chattering frantically, straight at the line of desperate fleeing Russians. They had done it. *SS Assault Regiment Wotan was moving again!*

CHAPTER 5

SURPRISINGLY ENOUGH it was the little Jew Pegleg Izzy who volunteered to enter the Russian village. Wrapping himself in a white camouflage smock taken from a panzer grenadier as a kind of white flag, the former knicker-elastic salesman hobbled towards the collection of straw-roofed cottages just as he might well have done in his old days on the road, gaze cast warily for angry dogs and angrier husbands with a score to pay from his last visit.

Behind him the Tiger crews waited, gunners already poised behind their machine-guns. But the men of the Wotan hoped that the place was held by their own troops. It had been a long tiring day since they had escaped from the ambush, and they were hungry and worn. Besides, their fuel was beginning to run out; and without fuel the sixty-ton monsters were useless tin cans.

'For a frigging Hebrew Jew, he ain't a bad sort of a swine,' the Butcher proclaimed proudly, as he watched his protégé hesitate at the first *isba* and then push on towards the square, with its usual House of Culture and onion-roofed church. 'Not a bad sort of swine at all.'

'But what would the Führer say?' Schulze said mockingly. 'A Hebrew Jew in his own SS! Think of that, Sergeant-Major.'

The Butcher poked a finger like a small pork sausage at his chest and growled. 'In this regiment, I decide who's a frigging Hebrew Jew or not, Schulze! You've been risking your lip a little too often of late.'

Before Sergeant Schulze could 'risk his lip' again, Matz cried, 'There he is – and he's got somebody with him on a bike. Holy strawsack, he's got a sword on as well!'

A few metres away the Vulture lowered his binoculars with a mild groan. 'My God, they're Rumanians!' he exclaimed in disgust. 'You can already smell the stink of scent and I shouldn't be surprised if he's not wearing a corset like they all do. Pederasts and piss-pansies, the lot of them!' He screwed his monocle more firmly into his right eye and glared at the little hobbling Jew and the officer riding the bike, his sabre trailing in the mud behind him.

Von Dodenburg nodded his silent agreement. If Paulus's Sixth Army, preparing for the bold thrust towards Stalingrad, had to rely for its protection on the left flank on these comic-opera soldiers, it would be in trouble if the Popovs ever counter-attacked.

But if the Rumanians of the First Royal Hussars were not much in the way of soldiers, they were good hosts. One hour later, the officers of SS Assault Regiment Wotan were being royally dined by the Rumanians in the House of Culture, served by waiters in white coats who bowed each time they presented a course.

The NCOs fared well too. 'Shit on shingle!' Matz exclaimed as he lined up outside the Hussars' kitchen and saw the food the smiling, dark-haired cooks had prepared for them. 'Look at the grub his lot get! None of yer frigging Old Man* for them. And look, Schulze, they even get free dago red! Give me half a chance and I'll volunteer for the Royal Hussars, even if they do ride shitting push-bikes!' Delighted beyond measure, he drained half the canteen of rough Rumanian red wine and grabbed an extra sausage from the great steaming tray, commenting, 'This is the frigging life!'

Schulze was not altogether convinced, though; for he had other things on his mind than just food, excellent though it was. 'Ask them, Matzi, which can has got the cunt in, willya?'

The Butcher, thanks to his new friend, had already found that particular source of delight, though it did not come in cans. 'The officers have a whore,' Pegleg Izzy whispered as the two of them stood behind the House of Culture, the Butcher striking a pose, with his hands on his hips, legs apart,

*Tinned meat, reputedly made from old men who had died in Berlin's workhouses

watching the men filing away to their billets with their canteens of food.

'Just one of them for all that lot?' the Butcher cried, already feeling that faint stirring of lust in his loins.

'She is a very big girl, Comrade Sergeant-Major,' Pegleg said by way of explanation. 'Italian. She was left here by them when they passed through. She has had plenty of experience.' The little ex-peddlar, who had lost his left leg to an enraged Cossack husband who had discovered him one afternoon doing more than just selling knicker-elastic to his wife, winked knowingly.

The Butcher stroked his ugly chin thoughtfully. 'A spaghetti-eater, eh. They say they're even better than the frogs. Up to all sorts of piggeries. Does she blow trombones, Izzy?'

'*Trombones!*' the little man exclaimed and rolled his cunning dark eyes towards the darkening sky, as if appealing to God himself. 'She blows *a whole orchestra* . . . I think.'

The Butcher thought of his failure in Paris and that unfortunate episode at the frontier which had brought the little 'Hebrew Jew' into his life and said, 'You know Izzy, you spoiled something for me that day, back at the border.'

'*O veh, o veh!*' Izzy moaned, swaying back and forth dramatically, as he recalled his father the *kantor* doing in the synagogue in the old days. 'Can you forgive me, Comrade Sergeant-Major?'

'All right, don't have a period, Izzy,' the Butcher snapped, the realisation growing on him that this might well be the last chance he'd get to solve his little problem before the great attack commenced. 'How can yer make it up to me, that's the question now?' He looked challengingly at the little man.

'I have already spoken to her of you,' Izzy stated, thrusting out his skinny little chest. 'I have told her of my friend, the general. *General Metzger!*'

The Butcher looked impressed. 'General, eh?'

'Of course. Low women of that kind are always impressed by men of rank and stature.' For a moment Izzy remembered his own days of glory before the Cossack had sawn off his leg with a meat-cleaver, when he had played the role of doctor with the simple peasant women. How they had enjoyed those little sessions of touching and feeling back in the haybarns when he had 'examined' them! 'And naturally *dallas*,' he added hastily, gesturing with his fingers as if he were counting money. 'She's sick of their Rumanian *lei*. She wants a hard currency like the Reichmark.'

The Butcher guffawed coarsely, and grabbed his flies. 'It won't be only hard currency she'll be getting, Izzy, mark my words! Now, *how* and *when?*'

'*Now*, while the officers are eating. They usually take their turns with her after they have eaten, the younger ones at least. Most of the older ones seem to prefer the mess waiters. I shall lead you to her. You will pay her for her services and the rubber overcoat, while I guard the door to ensure you are not disturbed.'

Hugely pleased, the Butcher slapped the little man heartily on the back and nearly knocked him off his pegleg. 'Got my own Parisian, Izzy. Good German stuff, none of this foreign muck; Type *Vulkan*. Can't take any risks with these whores.'

Pegleg Izzy nodded his old head sagely. 'Right you are, Comrade Sergeant-Major. The kind of diseases these Rumanians have, you'd end up carrying it around in a little cotton bag for the rest of your days.'

The Butcher winced as if in pain and snapped, 'Don't even say things like that. Now lead on. I'm as randy as an old billy-goat,' he added, lying somewhat in his enthusiasm, but optimistic as always.

Pegleg Izzy bowed like a waiter ushering a rich and respected customer into a restaurant. 'This way, Comrade Sergeant-Major . . . this way.'

So they walked through the thick black mud towards the little house conveniently situated behind the House of Culture, neither of them knowing that this was going to be a historic night; for this night Pegleg Izzy would save SS Assault Regiment Wotan and would become the only Jew ever to be awarded the Iron Cross (admittedly only the second class version of that medal for bravery) *from no less a person than Reichsführer SS Heinrich Himmler himself!*

> *'Tutto le sere, sotto quel fanal*
> *presso la caserne . . .*
> *Con ti Lili Marlene,*
> *Con ti Lili Marlene . . .'*

She had been crooning, lying on her back with her legs already spread and no knickers on, munching chocolates, as he had knocked and announced the '*Herr General*'.

His friend Sergeant-Major Metzger had soon put a stop to that. 'Knock off that macaroni stuff!' he had barked, tossing his cap on the bed. 'And you – *out!* This is no place for you.' With that he had shut the door on Pegleg Izzy's face, leaving him now to guard it, which he did willingly in spite of the chill night wind. It was not every day that he was allowed the privilege of guarding an important person's privacy while he was engaged in a very serious act. Though, he mused as he stood there nursing the Butcher's machine-pistol, nothing very much seemed to be happening. But then perhaps the Germans were gentlemen in bed, quiet and well-behaved, not noisy pigs like your average Russian. He smiled benignly and hoped his friend was enjoying it, whatever he and the Italian whore were doing at this moment behind the door.

Now night had fallen and silence had descended upon the remote village. Here and there there was the rusty squeak of one of the Rumanians' cycles as a sentry rode out on patrol, true to the tradition of the Hussars although they had long lost their horses. As for his new friends of Wotan, this night they were depending on the Rumanians for protection; for the most part, exhausted after the long day and filled to the brim with the coarse red Rumanian wine, they snored happily in their straw. Pegleg Izzy closed his eyes and dozed off leaning against the wooden frame of the whore's house.

It was the light *chink*, as if something metallic had snagged on wire, which awakened him. He opened his eyes with a start and stared into the inky darkness, his nostrils already assailed by an animal smell, raunchy and unpleasant, that he could not quite define. All he knew was that there was something out there in the inky darkness which he didn't like. Slowly the small hairs on the back of his skinny neck started to stand erect with fear . . .

Von Dodenburg dreamed. As always these days his dreams were violent and confused. He saw the faces of the boys he had shot once more, the jumbled horror of the turret when he had been wounded, the electric drama of trying to free the Tiger before they were overrun – and then suddenly the confusion became clarity and there she was. Claudine Louis. They had just made love, he knew that because there was a bed – a great old-fashioned brass bed – somewhere in the background of his dream, and he felt hot and flushed as if he had just experienced an orgasm.

But it was her lovely French face that dominated the dream, that and a conversation. 'Let us pretend,' she said sweetly, touching his cheek and smiling, 'let us pretend we are in a novel, you and me. Gallant *Boche* officer and patriotic French resistance girl . . . Somewhere, a long time in the future, there will be someone writing us into the story.' Again she had laughed and he had laughed with her, though he had not known why. 'What will he – this author – make us do, think, feel, eh?'

He shook his head and said he didn't know.

'I'd love you of course – in the novel,' she added hastily, 'but, of course, my first duty would be to France. *La patrie!* So what could – would – the ending of that kind of story be? Are you following me, Kuno?'

'Just.'

'Would it be a tragedy . . . or would there be a happy ending after all?' she persisted.

'The writer could write the ending any way he liked,' he answered. For now he knew what she was driving at.

'Tut tut!' she chided him, wagging her finger, staring him into thought with those fine dark Provençal eyes of hers. 'It's not that easy. Don't they say that characters in novels have lives of their own after a while? They say too that writers usually lose control of their books half-way through, so . . .'

He looked away.

She persisted and now he saw her breasts in the dream, fine, brown and heavy-nippled. He reached out a hand to touch them, and bring this conversation to its inevitable end. She pushed his hand from her and said. 'Let's think it out first, Kuno . . . The ending, which way is our life going to end – in the novel . . ?'

The first crazy chatter of a machine-pistol and the howl of some dying animal thrust von Dodenburg out of his sleep with a start. One moment later the whole world seemed to tremble and Claudine Louis and her 'ending' disappeared as if she had never even been there in the first place.

'*A real genuine blue-veiner!*' The Butcher cried in ecstasy, staring down in wonder as the Italian whore finally did the trick. 'All these months and now it's there! A diamond-cutter of the first water!'

The toothless whore redoubled her efforts, the sweat trickling down her fat back. She had been at it half an hour already and the Rumanians would be coming over soon. What stubborn men these *Tedesci* were! And she had even taken out her precious false teeth, unobtainable in this arsehole of the world if she lost them, in order to work him over better.

'I'm coming,' the Butcher gasped. 'Honest. . . I'm coming . . . *Schnell, Mädchen, schnell!*'

It was then that that same tremendous explosion which had awakened von Dodenburg ripped the very bed from beneath the two struggling, sweat-lathered lovers and in an instant all was total confusion as the naked whore grabbed her precious teeth, stuffing them in her mouth before rushing outside where Pegleg Izzy was firing yet another wild burst at those shadowy animals, bearing their deadly cargo, which seemed to be everywhere now.

For one instant, lying there in the midst of that wrecked bed, the Butcher stared sadly at his now flaccid organ, mumbling to himself, 'A real genuine blue-veiner.' And then he too was running, as everywhere the whistles shrilled and hoarse-voiced, angry NCOs cried in sudden alarm, 'Stand to . . . stand to . . . *we're being attacked!*'

Now the grim hunt commenced. The Royal Hussars had quickly disappeared, once they learned just how the village was being attacked by those silent, four-legged killers. But the killers were not after them. They had been trained to knock out one object only, and that was an armoured vehicle. They were hunting for the Tigers. A desperate Vulture, pistol in hand, ran back and forth through the glowing darkness, frantically trying to set up a firing line between the Tigers harboured beyond the House of Culture and this insidious enemy.

Von Dodenburg, commanding the other half of line, knew just how serious the situation was too. The little Jew's panted explanation and the first sight of that severed dog's head, ripped from its body by the explosion of the mine it had carried on its back, had soon convinced him that they were being attacked by a totally new weapon.

These half-wild dogs knew no fear. Trained by some means or other (he could not reason out how), they headed unhesitatingly towards the nearest tank. On their furry backs they bore the mines, with the detonator, a little metal rod like a radio aerial, whipping back and forth until it touched steel – and that was that. Nothing could stop the beasts – only death; and already they had blown the tracks off one Tiger and crippled it for good. Soon more of the metal monsters would end up the same way, if they didn't maintain a tight, an absolutely tight, firing line in front of them and knock off the alsatians at a safe distance.

'There, sir!' Schulze cried wildly, still only clad in his helmet and boots. '*To the right, over there!*'

Von Dodenburg spotted the dog. It was trying to sneak by the onion-roofed church, heading for the tanks with lemming-like determination. He fired a quick burst. The dog howled with pain and sank to its haunches. But still it attempted to crawl.

'Frig this for a tale!' Schulze yelled in anger and lobbed a stick grenade at the dying, crawling animal. It disappeared in a ball of fire as both the grenade and the mine attached to its body exploded in a great roar. All around, the Wotan troopers ducked hastily as debris flew everywhere.

But there were still more of them, crawling out of the darkness, howling with pain when they were hit, but still crawling on regardless until a shot hit their mines and they were blown into extinction.

Another one slipped through the firing line. Behind the angry, frightened, cursing men, a Tiger sank dramatically to one side in a burst of flame, its rear bogie blown right off, its severed track reeling out behind it like a broken limb.

In the end, it was only the flame-throwers that saved the day: a handful of terrified Rumanian Hussars, covered by the SS, advancing behind a wall of fire which even the killer dogs would not brave. Howling, snarling, baring their teeth like the savage wolves from which they were descended, they retreated slowly but surely until finally the darkness swallowed the survivors up, leaving the exhausted troopers to count the cost.

It was high: three Tigers had been knocked out completely, burning hulks now, beyond repair, and five had been severely damaged. Worst of all, the Rumanian fuel dump, on which they were going to rely to take them the rest of their way to their assembly point for the great surprise attack, had burned out. As the Vulture summed it up savagely, angrily kicking what was left of one of the dogs, 'They've done worse damage to the Regiment, von Dodenburg; than those shitting Gulag criminals of theirs. Much worse!' He whacked his cane against his blood-stained boot.

Von Dodenburg nodded his agreement miserably. Without a completely mobile and up to strength SS Assault Regiment Wotan to guard his flank, Paulus would not attack. 'The push will have to be postponed, sir, I suppose?'

'Yes, very definitely. Now it'll be the Popovs' turn,' he barked angrily and slapped his boot once again. *'God in heaven, when will I ever earn those damned general's stars . . ?'*

PART THREE

Ride Of Death

'Into the valley of death rode the gallant six hundred'.
Tennyson: The Charge of the Light Brigade.

CHAPTER 1

THE ALARM came on Paulus's Sixth Army front at dawn.

Around the lake the panzer grenadiers and other infantry lay in their trenches, miserable, cold and not a little frightened. As always at this time of day they stood to for half an hour, while the officers and NCOs did their rounds, just in case the Russians attacked. Thereafter, if they didn't, they would wash, eat, check their weapons and begin another long day of pushing slowly forward as Paulus had planned.

Ten minutes passed . . . twenty minutes . . . Already the veterans among the waiting Germans began sniffing the cold morning air in anticipation. Surely that was the delicious scent of 'nigger-sweat' being prepared by the kitchen bulls on their goulash cannons* somewhere to the rear? Twenty-five minutes passed. The officers commenced looking at their watches. In five minutes they'd stand the men down. Hopefully they'd get a chance of a good wash-down this morning? All of them smelled like unwashed monkeys. Six thirty.

A crack. A sudden hush. On the other side of the lake a flare hissed with frightening abruptness into the lightening sky. Almost instantly, the whole scene was bathed in an awesome red-glowing, light.

'*Stand by, men . . ! stand by, men . . !*' The urgent commands flew from hole to hole. Officers shouted orders. NCOs shrilled their whistles in red-faced fury. Hastily the German soldiers pulled off their right gloves and curled stiff fingers around their triggers, eyes narrowed for the first sight of the enemy. Adrenaline pumped new energy into their tired bodies. *The Popovs were coming!*

Nothing happened! For what seemed an age there was a

*Slang for mobile cooking ovens

nerve-racking silence. Desperately the defenders swallowed hard and peered into the new morning, hearts thumping away. Where were the bastards? What were they up to? The Ivans had to come soon – they had to!

Then it happened. The whole horizon seemed to erupt with earth-brown life. For one long moment the German defenders were paralysed with shock. They could not believe the evidence of their own eyes. Arms linked, singing and cheering, their flags waving bravely in the dawn wind, battalion after battalion of Soviet infantry were advancing on them! There were hundreds of them – *thousands* – stamping forward as if they were parading through Red Square, their mounted bayonets glistening like silver on that living wall. 'God in heaven,' the officers cursed, rubbing their red-rimmed eyes, 'it's not possible! There . . . *there must be a whole regiment of them!*'

But those German officers, who would not survive this dawn, were wrong. It was not a whole regiment attacking the 300 men dug in on the lake, but a whole division; and behind them waited two other divisions, ready to take up the attack if their comrades of the 343rd Rifle Division failed to break through.

Now the Russian officers waved their sabres. The division broke into a clumsy run. Arms still linked, crying a deep terrifying '*Urrah*', they split and ran to left and right of the lake straight for the German positions.

Hastily the German officers recovered from their shock as this cheering human avalanche descended upon them, 'Wait for it, men,' they urged, keeping their voices low and calm with professional deliberateness, although they knew their position was hopeless. 'Wait till you see the whites of their eyes.'

'I'd rather see the brown of their arses, sir!' would come back the sneer of the 'old hares'.*

But most of the men were too tense even to talk. Now they saw

*Veterans

and heard everything with a kind of tense electric clarity that they had never known before. Of course, the old hares could have told them why: this morning they were going to die. Desperately, before death overtook them, their brains wanted to register these last precious seconds on earth, pack everything in, before it was too late.

'Prepare to fire!' the officers ordered, some of them making a great show of studiously puffing at their cigars, as the earth-brown tide raced forward to submerge them for good.

Everywhere the riflemen and machine-gunners hunched over their weapons, knowing it was hopeless, yet praying fervently that it wasn't and that by some miracle they would survive this dawn. None of them would.

Suddenly the officers threw away their calm, their cigars, and dropped into the nearest holes, crying hurriedly as they did so, '*FIRE!*'

The machine-guns burst into hysterical life. A moment later the other weapons followed, joining that infernal stuttering concert. To their front, mines began to explode everywhere as the first wave ran into them and into that deadly fire which swept them away as if by the cruel strokes of a gigantic, invisible scythe. The second wave also disappeared. But the third came on, clambering over the dead bodies of their comrades, teeth bared like wild animals, eyes glazed and glaring with inhuman rage, their boots slipping and sliding on the bloody, jellied flesh of the dead.

Now the two lines clashed. Teeth shone white in powder-black faces. Eyes gleamed like those of the demented. Field-grey and Ivan fought, screaming terrible obscenities at each other. Now they chopped, slashed, tore, gouged, ripping at one another's bodies in atavistic fury. Rifles were useless now. They were replaced by knives, bayonets, shovels, knives, boots – bare hands. For a while it seemed that the Germans might hold the vital position. Once they even managed to regain lost ground. But then another wave submerged them for good and it was all over: *the line was broken!*

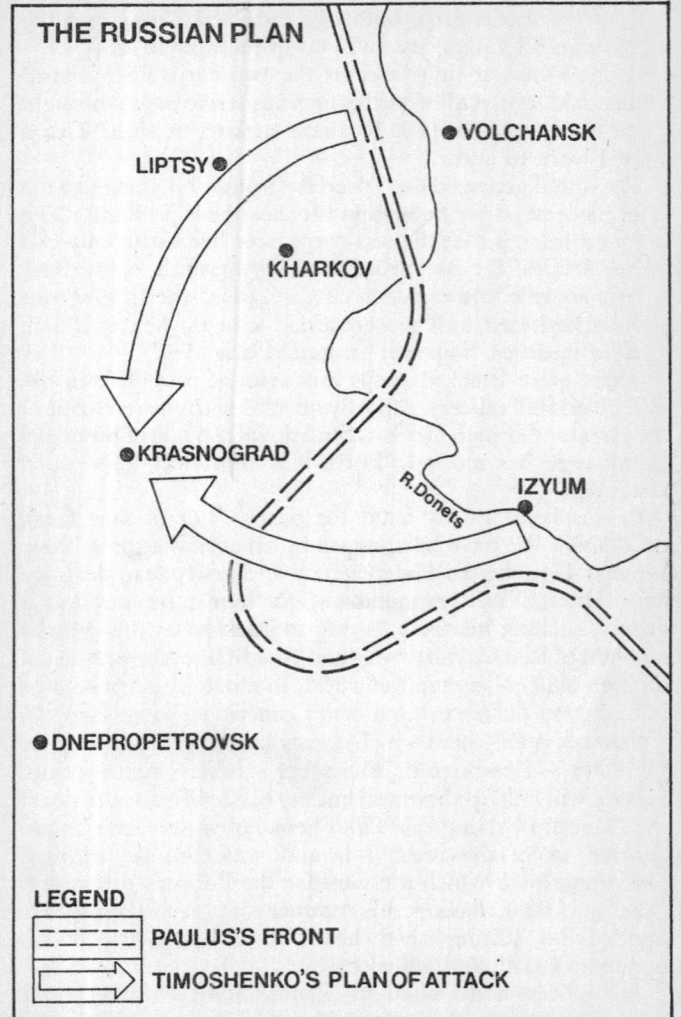

THE RUSSIAN PLAN

● VOLCHANSK

LIPTSY ●

● KHARKOV

← KRASNOGRAD

R. Donets

IZYUM

● DNEPROPETROVSK

LEGEND

═ ═ ═ ═ ═ PAULUS'S FRONT

⟹ TIMOSHENKO'S PLAN OF ATTACK

said, '*Herr Generaloberst*, both our own VII Corps and the Rumanian VI Corps, six divisions of infantry in all –'

'I know how many divisions the two corps have, man!' Paulus said testily, allowing his nervousness to break through. 'How many corps are the Russians striking us with? *That* is what I want to know.'

The Intelligence colonel peered through his glasses at the little piece of paper he held in his clawlike right hand. 'The latest estimate is that the two corps have been struck by two Soviet armies, the Sixth and the Fifty-Seventh, comprising twenty-six rifle and eighteen cavalry, plus,' the Intelligence Colonel hesitated, as if he were afraid to be the bearer of such terrible statistics, 'fourteen armoured brigades.'

There were shocked gasps and cries of protest from the assembled staff officers. A portly general with the red stripe of the Greater German General Staff down the side of his baggy riding breeches snorted, 'But this is absolutely impossible! *Impossible!*' ·

Paulus held up his hand for peace. 'Let us face facts, gentlemen. We have been struck by an overwhelming blow. What is Timoshenko's intention now?' He strode to the huge map. His staff officers made way for him as he stared at it grimly, sucking his teeth, trying to guess what that former sergeant of Red Cavalry, who had caught him, the product of the best staff colleges in the world, so much by surprise, was planning to do next. 'One of his pincers striking from the Volchansk area – here – is obviously heading through Liptsy for – say – Krasnograd. The other – here – starting from Izyum, will link up there and cut my Sixth off on both sides of the Donets. By doing this Timoshenko obviously feels he can deprive us of the road, rail and water routes through Dnepropetrovsk which are vital for the Führer's attempt to drive into the Caucasus this summer and on to the oil.' He nodded his distinguished head, as if approving of his opponent's skill, and fell silent.

His officers too waited in silence. Somewhere a phone jingled urgently and an affected but highly alarmed Prussian

voice was saying, 'But, man, you can't be right? They can't have got *that far* . . .!'

Paulus cleared his throat. 'This is now the question. Our front is broken everywhere. It is not surprising against such numbers. Do we try to stop the rot and call off our own offensive towards Stalingrad? Or do we attempt to please the Führer and continue the proposed drive as planned, and at the same time try to halt Timoshenko?'

His officers shuffled their feet nervously. Was this a serious question, they asked themselves? Was he playing with them? Of course he should call off the drive to Stalingrad and try to stop the rot on the Sixth Army front before it was too damned late!

But these men with their red-striped breeches did not know their Führer Adolf Hitler; nor did they fully realise the vanity of their commander. How could they know what was going through his mind at that moment as he began to take the momentous decision which would ensure his own complete disgrace and be the start of the Reich's downfall in Russia?

The Führer would never tolerate the cancelling of his vaunted offensive towards the Caucasus, Paulus could see that with the clarity of a vision. *His* plans were always right; they could never be halted. And some of his own vanity played a role too. Could an ignorant peasant, who once had not even possessed a pot to piss in, catch him, Paulus, off guard and beat him? Of course not! His family had been fighting for Prussia for three centuries. He had absorbed tactics and strategy with his mother's milk!

'No, *meine Herren*, we will *not* call off our attack. We attack as planned, with this slight change. It will be a single-pronged thrust in the area south of Izyum – here.'

'And the Russians?' the portly general with the red stripes gasped. 'Do we just let them carry on? *Herr Generaloberst*, they might not stop till they get to Berlin, damnit!'

Paulus forced a laugh, as if he were amused by the fat general's purple-faced indignation. 'My dear General,' he said condescendingly, 'don't you realise? The further

Timoshenko pushes forward, the longer and more vulnerable his flank will be.'

The fat general was not impressed. 'You mean, *Herr Generaloberst*, you intend to catch the Russians in the flank when they have extended themselves enough.'

'Exactly!' Paulus was very pleased with himself, now that he had managed to restore outward calm, at least, at his HQ. There was a lot of hard work ahead yet, he knew, before he would manage to patch up the terrible situation; but the first requisite was steady nerves, and his staff officers possessed those now.

'But with what, if I may be so bold as to ask, *Herr Generaloberst?*'

'You may. I have a combat-ready regiment, equipped with Tigers, on its way to the front at this moment. And fifteen minutes ago Marshal Antonescu* offered me a reserve division of Rumanian cavalry.'

'But, *Herr Generaloberst*, Rumanians and one regiment of tanks – I ask you!' the fat general objected, still unconvinced.

'They are of the SS, the tankers. They are the equivalent of one complete *Wehrmacht* panzer division, we all know that.'

'SS or not, they will be slaughtered.'

Paulus shrugged easily. 'Isn't that what the scum of the SS are there for, *Herr General?*' he asked cynically and dismissed the matter with a wave of his elegantly manicured hand. 'Now, gentlemen, let us have a closer look at this single thrust to Stalingrad. I suggest that we . . .'

So he planned, vain and arrogant, eager for glory, that fatal stroke which would bring Germany to its knees . . .

*The Rumanian Dictator

CHAPTER 2

THE BLOOD-RED ball of the sun was beginning to set on that endless steppe. From far away there came the muted rumbles of the heavy guns. They were mixed with deep drumroll of an electric storm approaching. Already the air was beginning to become thick and charged with electricity. Lightning stabbed the lowering sky an angry violet.

In the turrets of the waiting tanks, the men fidgeted nervously, irritated by both what was to come and the sticky air. Here and there they scratched at the lice awakened to new activity by the warmth. Some urinated over the sides of their turrets in bright yellow streams. Nobody spoke much; they were too tense. The radios were silent too; for the Vulture had ordered complete radio silence six hours before. He was not going to alert the Russians by any unusual wireless activity

To their right, silhouetted stark black against the setting sun, a troop of Rumanian cavalry started to push forward into the empty steppe, the hooves of their horses muffled so that they moved silently like gliding ghosts. They would cover the tanks' flank against any Russian infantry that might be lying in wait out there. Lightning stabbed the air again, a jagged fork splitting the sky to their immediate front. The burning ball howled to the earth, followed by the roar of thunder, bursting against their eardrums like a heavy barrage.

Von Dodenburg looked at his watch for the umpteenth time. Still ten minutes to go. God, why couldn't it all start, the terrible drama of battle, and let it be done with! This God-awful waiting was always the worst. Next to him in the hot, stuffy turret, Schulze bent down solemnly and shook hands with Matz in the driver's compartment. No words were exchanged, but von Dodenburg knew what the two old running-mates were thinking. This was their kind of parting.

He frowned, suddenly reminded of the killing to come. A single regiment, plus the Rumanians, hopelessly out-dated and badly led, against the whole weight of the Popovs' flank. It didn't bear thinking about. He looked at his watch again. Still two minutes to go.

One hundred metres away, the Vulture also looked at his watch. The new *Sonderführer*, Pegleg Izzy, now officially interpreter and prisoner interrogator to the SS Assault Regiment Wotan, proudly did the same. He was learning fast from these Germans who had adopted him, now that he was going to be awarded the medal. Already he was learning to strike his wooden leg with a switch, just as Colonel Geier did. Soon he would learn a lot more from them. He smiled winningly at his friend, Sergeant-Major Metzger. But the Butcher was too miserable and scared to return the look. He stared in glum dread at the darkening horizon. Pegleg Izzy straightened his new armband with its '*Sonderführer*' and swastika and told himself that the Sergeant-Major was too eager for the action to come to notice a lowly person like himself.

More Rumanian cavalry, some of them bearing long lances, started to trot noisily to the flanks. So far there was no sign that the Russians, if they were out there somewhere, had noticed the Rumanians. Perhaps, if they had, they took them for patrols. Perhaps they didn't even care. Rumanians? – *so what*.

The Vulture's finger tightened around the trigger of his signal pistol. Thirty seconds to go. Of course, any officer with a modicum of sense would know that the Wotan would be decimated in this attack against the Russian flank – they were hopelessly outnumbered. Who was he, though, to question the decisions of army commanders? The main thing was that he achieved the glory of this bold attack and that in due course he would be awarded his general's stars. He drew a deep breath, flashed a last look at his watch, and as the storm broke in all its fury, pressed the trigger of his raised signal pistol.

A crack, a hiss, a soft plop. The green flare sailed effortlessly into the wild, crazy air. As one, a thousand or more faces turned upward to the first raindrops, suddenly turned a glowing, eerie green in the reflected light, eyes filled with awe, as if they had just seen a benevolent God descending from the heavens in the company of all His archangels.

But this was the God of War, come to fetch them for the bloody, savage battle to come, from which so few of them would emerge; and He brooked of no delay.

'*Start up!*' the young commanders, eager for this desperate glory, cried on all sides, as if they could not die quickly enough. Everywhere along that long line, the drivers pressed their buttons hastily.

Thin blue smoke started to stream out of the Tigers' exhausts. A throaty cough, a protesting grunt and then with an ear-splitting roar the first mighty engine burst into life. The next followed. And the next. In an instant the thick, brooding silence was shattered, made hideous with noise. Abruptly the clean air was sickly with fumes.

The Vulture flashed a proud look to left and right, arms outspread, holding the sides of the command vehicle with his gloved hands. Behind him Pegleg Izzy, face streaming with raindrops, proudly did the same. He was satisfied with what he saw. The young fools couldn't wait to die. He waved his cane above his head and cried above the racket, '*Roll 'em!*'

'*Roll 'em . . . roll 'em . . .*' The hoarse excited cry was taken up from turret to turret. '*ROLL 'EM!*'

With a rusty, metallic creak, as if the big steel monsters were reluctant to move, the Tigers started to lurch forward, their decks piled with rain-washed, excited panzer grenadiers in their camouflaged smocks and helmets, laughing crazily now, shouting jokes and taunts at each other above the racket, going into action.

Sergeant Schulze shook his head. 'Lambs to the slaughter,' he repeated to no one in particular. 'Shitting young innocent lambs!' Then he squatted behind that monstrous 88mm gun and prepared for what must surely come.

Behind them there was an earth-shaking roar which drowned the noise of the tanks and the storm. With a hoarse, exultant scream, the whole weight of the Rumanians' artillery hurtled over their heads like scores of express trains going all-out, to explode with a tremendous smack on the horizon in front of them. Suddenly it was burning everywhere. Even at that distance, the awed panzer grenadiers gasped for breath, as that tremendous heat scorched their tonsils, snatched the very air from their lungs and had them gasping and choking like old men in the throes of a fatal seizure.

Now the line of steel was wading forward through the steppe-grass in a great extended V, behind that wall of moving fire, with, on the flanks, the Rumanian cavalry, clearly outlined by the flames, spreading out ever further to left and right. Everything was going smoothly. So far not a single shot had been fired at them. It was obvious: no one could live in that blazing hell!

But they could!

Suddenly the Rumanian cavalry to the right were spurring their horses into a wild gallop, throwing away their lances in their efforts to achieve speed, returning the way they had come, the riders bent low over their flying mounts, whipping them mercilessly ever faster, as if the devil himself were behind them. Machine-guns started to chatter; those slow antiquated Russian machine-guns. Now everywhere the Rumanians were being shot off their horses, throwing up their arms in melodramatic agony, going down under the flying hooves, being dragged on, feet caught in their stirrups, crushed beneath falling mounts which whinnied piteously as the scarlet streaks of their own blood patched their sweat-lathered sides.

'Popovs, ' Schulze, squinting through his sight, announced almost sadly, as if he had known all the time this would happen. 'Frigging scores of them . . . Now the clock is really in the piss-pot!'

'Can we not have a little more military formality, Sergeant

Schulze?' Von Dodenburg matched the big sergeant's sangfroid with his own. 'Let us report in a correct regulation fash –'

But there was no need for Schulze to report. To his immediate right front a light burned a bright white-zinc. The air was torn apart like a piece of gigantic canvas being violently ripped. A bright white blur hurried towards them at a tremendous rate. The Tiger reeled. For an instant the turret glowed a deadly, frightening purple as the armour-piercing shell grazed along it, trying – in vain – to find a way in, and then it was howling off uselessly and the battle could commence . . .

All that storm-racked night, the men of Wotan fought their way forward across the steppe, driving the surprised Soviets in front of them. But the Russians fought back bravely, making the SS pay the price for their victory – the Rumanians too. The steppe was littered with their corpses, and riderless horses, some of them pitifully wounded, wandering aimlessly everywhere, or stood cropping the grass next to their dead riders.

Dawn came. The red ball of the sun hung on the horizon, bathing the steppe an eerie orange and throwing everything into harsh, stark relief. The lead tanks paused. Hurriedly their crews began to drape the large black and red swastika flags over the decks. Other men sprang to the ground and started to unroll canvas arrows on the grass, pointing to their front where the unseen Russians were waiting for them to attack.

But again the Germans had a surprise in store for the enemy. Now all was ready and the weary, filthy men of the Wotan dipped their heads in pails of blessedly cool water and took huge gulps of cold 'nigger sweat' from their water bottles, holding them with hands that trembled visibly. No one ate. This morning their stomachs would not hold any food. Instead they smoked, devouring the 'lung torpedoes' greedily, sucking in the blue smoke, feeling the tobacco soothing their jingling nerves.

The Stukas came dead on time. One moment they were simply black specks on the horizon; the next they were hovering like sinister black hawks right over the German positions. Below, the Wotan troopers shaded their eyes against the oblique rays of the dawn sun and watched as their leader waggled his gull-like wings to indicate that he had recognized the German positions and was waiting for further instructions, while behind him his planes seemed to hover there like birds of prey waiting to dive on their unsuspecting quarry.

Now smoke grenades started to stream out from the German positions, hushing to where they suspected the Russians had dug in their tanks. Immediately they started bursting in the low foothills sending up streams of brilliant white smoke. The Stukas waited no longer. They moved forward, dragging their evil black shadows across the upturned faces of the watchers, heading for the enemy. The men of Wotan tensed, knowing what was soon to come.

Suddenly the leading Stuka dropped out of that burning sky. Motors and sirens howling frantically, the Stuka commander roared down, diving for the ground at five hundred kilometres an hour, seemingly bent on suicide, gravity pressing his body hard back against the armoured seat, his face behind the goggles flattened by the pressure, mouth wide open to prevent his eardrums being burst. Down and down! The green steppe leapt up to meet him at a tremendous rate. Gawping like village yokels, the troopers watched that tremendous ride of death. Surely nothing could save the crazy pilot from destruction.

At the very last moment the Stuka seemed to stop in mid-air. The watchers gasped. The black-painted plane staggered visibly. They could hear the metal fabric scream under the terrible strain. Then from its ugly belly a myriad tiny, lethal eggs started to fall, tumbling down towards the Russian positions in crazy, hectic confusion. Moments later the ground trembled and everywhere black earth tinged with flame and bits and pieces of what had once been human beings spewed upwards. The dive-bombing attack of Adolf Hitler's 'flying artillery' had commenced . . .

'Then – *roll 'em!*' the Vulture shrieked above that banshee-like howl and the thick, throaty *crump* of bombs. '*ROLL 'EM!*'

The Tiger crews needed no urging. They knew their lives depended upon hitting the Russian positions while they were still paralysed by the bombing attack. Their faces glazed with sweat, they thrust home their gears and the gigantic tanks began to roll into battle once again. Like primeval monsters, they lumbered forward towards that smoking, jumbled mess of twisted, torn equipment and ruined foxholes, their long overhanging 88mm cannon swinging slowly from side to side as if seeking their quarry.

'*T-34 – three o'clock!*' von Dodenburg cried above the racket, as he spotted the first enemy tank coming out of the black smoke. Automatically he opened his mouth against the blast to come.

'*On!*' Schulze yelled, bent over his gun.

'*FIRE!*' von Dodenburg shrieked.

The great tank shuddered. Matz fought the controls desperately as it reared back on its sprockets like a live thing. For an instant he caught a glimpse of the AP shell hissing from the gun. Then acrid yellow smoke whipped back against his tense face. Up above, the breech screamed back and a steaming yellow shell case came clattering to the deck. Automatically von Dodenburg pressed the smoke-extractor and craned forward eagerly, his face set in a wolfish grimace.

Slowly, very slowly, the Popov gunner was attempting to swing his own 75mm gun round, as thick white smoke poured from the T-34's engine. It was almost as if he were already slumped dying over the breech, trying to get off one last shot in his final, angered desperation.

But that wasn't to be. 'Brew him up!' von Dodenburg cried, carried away by that blood-lust of battle. '*BREW THE FUCKER!*'

Schulze fired again, the sweat pouring down his furrowed

brow. The T-34 trembled crazily. With majestic slowness its ten-ton turret sailed into the air. Next instant it jetted scarlet flame and disintegrated.

An inhuman something came staggering out of the flame, charred, blackened shrivelled, one hand outstretched like a burned twig in front of it, as if pleading for mercy. But there would be no mercy on this new day of battle. Somewhere a machine-gun chattered frantically and the something reeled back, what looked like red buttonholes suddenly stitched in the charred black. Next instant von Dodenburg's tank rolled over the Russian and pulped him into his native earth.

One hour after the Stuka attack, the men of Wotan began to run into an improvised Russian defence line. It was as if some enemy commander had realised that Timoshenko's great thrust to the west would leave him with an extended flank and had decided to prepare for any German flank attack. Now the tanks everywhere began to bump into earth-bunkers, some equipped with 57mm anti-tank guns, and already that dreaded howl of the feared Russian 'Stalin Organ' could be heard on all sides. The Russian defence was thickening.

But the Vulture would not hear of any slowing down. 'Forward, damn you!' he barked time and time again into the radio. 'I will not have you bogging down! In three devils' name, *will you keep those men going!*'

Now they advanced through the Soviet rockets which screeched down from the 'Stalin Organs' trailing huge plumes of white smoke behind them, zig-zagging violently in bursts of black earth, each tank crew, nerves tingling electrically, on the alert for the first sign of an anti-tank gun; slowed down as they were in this shell-pitted, steaming lunar landscape, even the Tiger was vulnerable to a 57mm shell at close range. And all the time Soviet machine-gun bullets pattered against the tanks' steel sides like heavy tropical rain on a tin roof, keeping the crews boxed up in the hot, smoke-filled interiors of their sixty-ton monsters. As Schulze exclaimed angrily, 'If this goes on, sir, it's gonna cost the Reich twenty marks for me to have a little tomtit!'

And von Dodenburg knew what the irate NCO meant. Any one of the crew wanting to relieve himself now would have to fire a shell, worth twenty marks, in order to carry out his natural function; it was too dangerous to pop out of the tank for that kind of business. 'Do it down the side of the your leg, you big rogue!' he cried unsympathetically as the Tiger reeled with the impact of a near miss.

'Can't,' Schulze replied, his sweat-lathered, dirty face breaking into a grin. 'Done it –'

'*Anti-tank – three o'clock!*' Matz broke in with a shriek.

To their right, a 57mm cannon opened up at less than three hundred metres' range. A terrified von Dodenburg could actually see the white blur of the AP shell hurtling towards them.

But Matz reacted correctly. He spun the Tiger round as if it were a toy car. The big tank disappeared in a cloud of flying gravel and earth and the shell raced by them harmlessly.

Von Dodenburg, his mouth full of warm, copper-tasting blood where he had slammed against the turret due to that surprise manoeuvre, slapped Schulze on the shoulder angrily.

He needed no urging. 'Cheeky Popov prick!' he yelled and pressed the trigger of his machine-gun. The crew of the anti-tank gun went reeling, thrown back under the impact of that tremendous burst. Next moment Matz drove the Tiger straight at the gun. It disappeared, together with its crew, under those broad, churning tracks, to be flung out on both sides like red-raw pieces of chopped beef.

A T-34 shell whizzed by them. The Tiger rocked, as if it were made of paper and not steel. A T-34 reared up right to their front. Momentarily its soft underbelly was visible as it breasted a shell-hole.

Schulze pressed his pedal. The turret spun round. His eyes flashed to the loading signal. It burned red. In the sight the twin triangles met. Right on target! Squatting next to him in the foul, hot turret, von Dodenburg could see every detail of the Soviet tank, down to the last rusty rivet.

Schulze pulled the firing lever. There was the clang of steel on steel. An enormous din like Thor smiting a gigantic anvil. The T-34 simply disappeared. One moment it was there; the next it was gone and they were rumbling forward through a steel rain, as the rent metal hurtled down.

It was about that time, just after they had blasted the T-34 to pieces, that the strangest incident of that whole long second day full of death, destruction and strange incidents, occurred. They had just cleared out another Soviet bunker by the simple expedient of racing the Tiger round and round above the trapped Ivans until they were choked to death by the exhaust fumes, when suddenly out of the smoke of war an ancient biplane came hurtling towards them, machine-guns spitting.

'Christ on a crutch!' Schulze cried, more in amazement than fear. 'A frigging sewing-machine's gonna have a go – *at us!*'

His surprise was justified. What could the 'sewing machine', a Rata, normally used for reconnaissance, do against the sixty-ton steel monster?

But the Russian tried. Time and time again, it buzzed around the lone tank, peppering it impotently with its bullets, coming down so low that twice its wings touched the ground. In the end von Dodenburg grew impatient of this impudent gadfly, which obviously had recognized from the Tiger's many aerials that it was a command tank. 'In God's name, Schulze, can't you knock the pig-dog out of the sky! It's getting on my nerves.'

'Exactly, sir. It's beginning to bring on my migraine too. Unless,' he grinned at the officer, 'I'm starting to get my monthlies.'

'Get on with it, man!'

Schulze kicked Matz on the right shoulder twice, the signal for 'slow-down'.

Obediently a weary Matz, his face covered with grease and

dust so that his eyes blazed from his face, white and startling like those of a 'nigger minstrel', did so.

Now Schulze followed the rickety old biplane as it came in low across the scorching steppe for yet another frustrating attack, the second airman, who acted as gunner, swinging his machine-guns round. 'Come on baby,' he whispered to himself, 'come to daddy now! Come on – *NOW!*'

His jaw clenched. He pressed the trigger. The turret machine-gun chattered into frenetic activity. A stream of tracer zipped towards the plane. Like lethal morse it hurtled between the stationary tank and the biplane. Watching in grim fascination, von Dodenburg saw the slugs slam into the plane's radial motor. The prop splintered immediately. Thick white glycol started to pour from the shattered engine. 'You've got him . . ! *you've got him!*' he cried joyously.

'I should be in the frigging Luftwaffe!' Schulze exclaimed and slumped back in his leather seat, as the pilot fought desperately to keep his plane in the air.

To no avail. It hit the ground with a spectacular slap. Its undercarriage splintered and broke off immediately. In a crazy skid, it slid across the surface of the steppe, trailing a wake of flying earth behind it. Frantically the pilot, clearly visible at the controls, tried to avoid the stunted trees and clumps of bushes. Several times he managed to do so, then his luck ran out. His left wing slammed into a gnarled old oak, broke off like a metal leaf and left the plane skidding round in a curve which almost overturned it, to come to a shuddering stop.

Abruptly all was silence.

But not for long. Von Dodenburg pressed his throat-mike excitedly. 'Come on, Matz, hit the tube! Let's be the first in the Wotan to claim they've shot down a plane. We need the pilot to prove it!' But that wasn't to be.

As the tank rumbled to a stop opposite the wrecked, smoking plane, the two crewmen, both clad in black leather tunics with helmets of the same material, stumbled dizzily from their plane, fumbling for their pistols.

'Watch it, sir!' Schulze urged, as von Dodenburg prepared

to spring down from the turret. 'The Popovs are gonna try to fight it out, the stupid cunts!'

'Give them a burst from the MG,' von Dodenburg commanded hastily.

Schulze pressed his trigger. Lead stitched the ground a dozen metres away from the two Russians now struggling with their pistols. But that furious burst did not deter them from their aim. In the same instant that von Dodenburg dropped from the turret, first the one, then the other pressed his pistol to his head and blew his brains out. Von Dodenburg stopped in his tracks . . .

One minute later they made their discovery. Matz, of course, was intent on finding a possible flatman of vodka when he made it. 'Come and look at this, sir,' he cried in amazement, wizened face suddenly ashen. 'They . . . they're . . .

'They're *what?*' von Dodenburg asked, turning from his examination of the wrecked plane and walking over to where the would-be looter knelt, transfixed as he stared down at the dead bodies.

'Women, sir . . .' Matz gasped. 'They're both *women* . . .!'

They were indeed. The bigger of the two had short-cropped hair, cut like a man's, but there was no mistaking the fact that she was a woman: her jacket had been forced open by the impact of the crash and now one large blood-stained breast thrust out of her shirt. Next to her, the other one had long blonde hair and her lips were painted red. They were women all right.

Schulze, standing next to von Dodenburg, whistled softly and said, almost as if to himself, 'If even the Popov womenfolk are gonna fight like that – then heaven help Germany!'

Von Dodenburg nodded silently. For the first time in three years of war, the tall, harshly-handsome Captain felt faint stirrings of unease and disquiet. First Claudine Louis on the other side of the continent, now these two unknown Russian women, dead by their own hands just like her. *Could Germany win against such people?*

CHAPTER 3

ALL THAT long terrible week they battered their way ever deeper into the Russians' flank, overcoming terrible odds, fighting for every kilometre of ground, their ranks growing ever thinner.

Now there was no difference any more between the 'old hares' and the greenbeaks. They were all veterans now, haggard, worn, unshaven, their eyes popping out of their heads like those of madmen. They stank of sweat, oil and death. Sleep was almost unknown. They moved day and night, catching a nap whenever they could. Food consisted of cold coffee and hunks of bread and sausage; for now, to make up his losses, the Vulture had ordered up all the rear echelon swine to take their places with the fighting men. This terrible week even Sergeant-Major Metzger found himself commanding a troop of Tigers – reluctantly.

The heat was tremendous. All day long the sun blazed down over that endless naked steppe, turning their tanks into ovens, bathing the plagued tankers in a hot sweat. Once they captured a village and ordered the firemen to douse their vehicle with water from the village pump by means of their ancient horse-drawn engine. For a few moments they became boys again, as the cool refreshing water doused their dirty, skinny bodies and ran down the sides of their vehicles. But within minutes the relentless heat had steamed their uniforms and tanks dry once more and the heat seemed even more intense.

Within that one short week, the war and Russia had completely brutalized them. They expected no mercy and gave none. Prisoners were not taken. What should they do with them anyway? Captured Russians were shot on the spot. The Soviets replied in kind. Twice they found their own dead, snatched from the column at night by marauding Cossacks or partisans, cruelly tortured and murdered. On the third occasion the Russians had nailed their prisoner to a barn door, put out his eyes with burning sticks and left him to die, with below him the legend in good German scrawled in chalk, '*CROAK, GERMAN – CROAK!*'

'Kill me, comrades,' the boy had choked when they found him. 'Oh please, comrades, for my mother's sake, kill me!' And tears had poured pitifully from those sightless holes.

The Vulture had shot him dead with his first bullet. That day the men of Wotan ran amok in a small newly-captured Russian village. It was completely spontaneous. No one gave an order. The men simply went wild, shooting and slaughtering, driving the screaming survivors before them – men, women and children – to be shot down against the wall of the House of Culture.

In vain, the officers tried to restore order. But the men were completely out of hand, setting fire to the miserable, straw-roofed huts, flushing out the Russians who had tried to hide there, slashing at them with their bayonets, cleaving their skulls with their entrenching tools, and screaming all the while like savage, mad animals. In the end it was, surprisingly enough, the little Jewish *Sonderführer*, Pegleg Izzy, who managed to restore some sort of order. He burst into a group of howling young panzer grenadiers attempting to thrust an ancient greybeard into the communal cesspit, waving a bottle and crying, 'There's vodka, comrades. . . lots of it, back there. . . Do you hear, comrades – *vodka!*' And that had done it.

Half an hour later the square was littered with drunken troopers, some already snoring fast asleep in the dirt next to the bodies of those they had so cruelly slaughtered; others weakly trying to pour more vodka down their throats, seeking that same boon of blessed oblivion.

'A bad business, von Dodenburg,' the Vulture said grimly, as the two of them walked through the looted, raped, tortured village, followed by the hobbling *Sonderführer*. 'A very bad business. The men are getting out of hand.'

'It's the pressure, sir.' Von Dodenburg tried to defend Wotan, taking his eyes off the woman, her skirts thrown up, her legs spread, with the trickle of already hardening black blood down the side of her leg: she had obviously been raped before she had been killed. 'The strain is too much for them. Remember, sir, that most of them are barely eighteen!' He bit his bottom lip and hastily stepped aside. *There was a headless baby in the gutter!*

Behind him Pegleg Izzy gasped and muttered something in a language that von Dodenburg could not understand. Perhaps it was a prayer for the baby; he hoped so.

'Do not think, von Dodenburg, I am concerned with their moral welfare,' the Vulture sneered. 'Those of them who might survive this war will be hopeless criminal scum anyway. The state will probably have to lock them up. They could not be trusted in civilised society – *our heroes!*' He looked contemptuously at the drunks lolling in the dust, clutching their bottles as if their very lives depended upon them. 'No, it is not that at all. I mean discipline to continue the fight, von Dodenburg. Look at the drunken pigs, what could they do now if the Russians launched a surprise attack, which thank God they won't? For the time being they've had a noseful.' He slapped his cane against the side of his dusty, battered boot. 'My dear Captain, I'll give them another – say – fourteen days and by then those who survive will be finished, spent as soldiers. No good for anything but shovelling shit in the rear – *or the funny farm!*'

In the days that followed, von Dodenburg came more and more to agree with his CO's prediction. The world had gone crazy and sometimes, as they battled ever onwards through that terrible country, he felt he was going crazy too, ripe for the Vulture's 'funny farm'.

Nothing seemed normal any more. Day was turned into night with smoke and the fog of war. Night was turned into day, lit by the fiery fury of exploding shells and burning villages. The men seemed drunk all the time; perhaps they were – on looted vodka. Accidents mounted rapidly. A boy walked into the moving tracks of a Tiger and was pulped to red death, almost as if he had wanted to be. Another went mad and had to be restrained. A day later the Pill put his service pistol inside his mouth and blew the back of his head off. No one knew why. It was a crazy time.

Even Schulze and Matz were not their usual selves. They were moody, morose, given to sudden outbursts of anger. Matz, who delighted in driving, especially this new wonder weapon, the Tiger, suddenly hated it. 'Frigging track!' he would cry in rage and slam his boot against the metal rungs when they became loose. 'Porsche – he should shove his frigging engine up his arse – *sideways!*' he'd bellow when yet again the new Porsche engine overheated.

Schulze lacked his old humour too. More than once, as the fighting erupted yet again and the order would come through, 'Prepare for attack – prepare for attack!' he would declare to no one in particular, 'Me, I hate the fucking world! One of these days, I'm gonna get that shovel from the side of this frigging can of sardines and take it for a frigging walk' – he meant go and defecate, for which a spade was necessary – '*and never frigging well, come back again!*'

'*They're falling apart, Obersturmbannführer!*' von Dodenburg protested to the Vulture more than once. 'They're living off their nerves . . . They can't go on much more like this – attacking day in, day out.'

The Vulture, his face unshaven, his boots powdered with white dust, even his monocle dirty, had not seemed to hear. '*March or croak* . . . march or croak, von Dodenburg, that is our motto these days,' he would reply invariably.

But in the end the Vulture had seen that they could not go on like this. It was the day they had been forced to abandon a group of twenty or so wounded, too serious to go on with the rest of the Regiment. They had lain in the dying rays of the evening sun, shading their eyes on their stretchers, as the Vulture gave them his usual parting speech reserved for such occasions: 'We are proud . . . your sacrifice will not be forgotten . . . Our Führer Adolf Hitler is surely a proud man today to know that . . . such bold young men . . . willing to give their all . . . for the holy cause of our Thousand Year Reich . . .' He had trotted out the usual empty phrases until he had come to that overwhelming, frightening truth, and even he seemed somehow embarrassed at what he was going to have to tell them. 'We shall have to leave you here – for a little while.' He indicated the empty, burned-out Russian hamlet which had cost them their limbs and which they had stormed so bravely. 'The Rumanians are sending up their doctors immediately. It could only be a matter of perhaps two hours before they reach you . . .' His voice trailed away to nothing as he saw the looks of alarm crossing their pale, shaken faces; those, that is, who were still conscious.

In two hours night would have fallen and the steppe would again belong to the Cossacks and the partisans. They knew it too, and what would happen to them if they fell into the Russians' hands. '*Obersturmbannführer*,' one of them called piteously, wringing his hands, the tears streaming down his wan face under the blood-stained bandage which circled his head, 'you can't leave us here . . . like that! You know, sir, what they will do to us when they come? Horrible things!' He shuddered dramatically and von Dodenburg turned his head away, unable to bear any more, mind full of those boys he had once killed himself in what seemed another age.

The Vulture's voice hardened into its old Prussian rasp. 'I just don't have the men to attend to you. Our doctor is dead, as you know. Now for God's sake, pull yourself together, man! Remember you are a German soldier!'

Suddenly it happened. Von Dodenburg heard the Vulture's sharp gasp of surprise and swung round. A blond giant, a bandage wrapped round his naked chest, had somehow risen from his stretcher and was advancing on the Vulture, face contorted crazily, stick grenade in his hand. '*Swine!*' he was saying, the saliva dribbling down the side of his chin. 'Swine . . . We fight for you . . . die for you . . . and now you abandon us . . . Cruel swine . . . *Now die!*' He raised his grenade and von Dodenburg could see he had already pulled the china pin; the thing was armed and ready to explode. '*DIE!*'

But the Vulture was not fated to die – just yet. With surprising agility for a cripple, Pegleg Izzy thrust out his wooden leg and caught the desperate man in mid-stride.

He stumbled and then sprawled full-length, the hissing grenade still clutched in the hand with which he had attempted to save himself.

'*Hit the dirt!*' von Dodenburg cried frantically and flung himself to the ground as the earth heaved beneath the blond giant and the grenade exploded, tearing his face off as if it were a blood-red mask.

For what seemed a long time, they simply lay there, shaking visibly, all of them. Then one by one, slowly, they rose, shaking their heads to get rid of the boom, trying to make their vision come back into focus.

The Vulture himself helped Pegleg Izzy to his feet. 'Thank you, Jew,' he said gravely, the old rasp vanished from his voice. 'You saved my life. I will not forget.'

Nor did he. When the Vulture and all of them present that evening were long, long dead, Pegleg Izzy would be still living on in one of Tel Aviv's poorer suburbs, boring anyone prepared to listen to his drunken stories about the days when he served with the SS and won his 'medal'.

Wearily the Vulture rubbed his eyes, as if he were very tired and had just realised it for the first time. 'Von Dodenburg, you are right and I was wrong. The men are falling apart. What just happened . . .' He shrugged. 'Stand the men down. We stay here. I shall take it up with the commanding general myself. It will be my responsibility. That is all.' He walked away, shoulders bent as if in defeat . . .

Twenty-four hours later the leading brigade of the Rumanian cavalry trotted through the lines of happy SS men lazing in the sun, too pleased with this unexpected break to jeer the miserable Rumanians who seemed to know what lay ahead for them on the horizon: *Trouble!*

They were not mistaken. That same afternoon the Rumanians ran bang-slap into a fortified position which the Russians had built along the line of foothills to the front of the Wotan. It stopped them dead.

CHAPTER 4

GENERALOBERST PAULUS looked hard at the collection of battle-scarred Tigers and the men sprawled in the grass around them. They were clean and shaven now and they had eaten a warm meal at last. But the horror and the fatigue had still not vanished from their haggard young faces. The long, hard battle for the flank was still with them. He nodded and looked down at the Vulture. 'I take your point, Geier,' he barked. 'Your men have done more than enough. Your losses in men and material have been high, I can see that.'

'Fifty per cent of the Regiment has fallen, *Herr Generaloberst*,' the Vulture replied guardedly, wondering all the time why he had been honoured so unexpectedly by the Army Commander personally. 'And we have had no replacements.'

'I understand . . . I understand fully, Geier,' Paulus repeated and the Vulture breathed an inner sigh of relief. At least he was not going to be sacked for having stood his regiment down without authorization.

The tall Commanding General paused beneath the shade of a stunted tree and peered towards the horizon where the guns were rumbling once more as the Rumanians tried yet another attack on the Russian positions. 'Do you know, Geier, I am within an ace of capturing Stalingrad. The single strike has paid off. The Russians won't be able to stop us up there now, I am confident of that.'

'Congratulations, sir,' the Vulture said warily.

Standing at a respectful distance, von Dodenburg frowned. Paulus was so obviously vain and cocksure. He had taken an instinctive dislike to the General.

A little further off, Schulze, lounging half-naked in the grass, running a glowing cigarette-end along the seams of his lice-ridden shirt, felt pretty much the same about Paulus. 'Yer can crap in yer hat, put it on yer head and call it frigging curls, Matzi!' he declared. 'But that big fart ain't up to no good, mark my words. It's buy combs, lads, cos there's lousy times ahead again.'

And Matz nodded his head in silent agreement. Why else did generals ever come to the front? Only to cause frigging trouble for the poor long-suffering stubble-hoppers.

'But there is a fly in the ointment, Geier,' Paulus was saying, standing there obviously enjoying a respite from the blazing sun. 'That damned hill position. Break through that and Timoshenko's flank attack will be split in two. Then he will be forced to break off his own thrust westwards and then we have him.' He screwed up his pale, well-manicured hand in a curiously weak and ineffectual gesture, von Dodenburg couldn't help thinking. 'He will have no other alternative but to retreat and that's the end of his hash.' He smiled cynically. 'But then, what does one expect from a man who started his military career as a bandy-legged sergeant of cavalry, eh, Geier?'

The Vulture nodded warily. He too had taken the measure of Colonel General Paulus. There was a definite flaw in his character. Inside, in spite of his great size and high rank, the man was decidedly weak. He waited for what was to come.

'The Rumanians will never take that hill line, you know, Geier,' Paulus stated flatly, as if it were just a fact of life. 'The men are ignorant peasants who haven't the faintest idea what they are doing in this God-forsaken country. Their officers are fops and pederasts.'

The Vulture looked at his boots and von Dodenburg hastily suppressed a grin. If the Colonel-General only knew to whom he was making his pronouncements!

'The only troops that will take that hill line are honest, solid German troops who know what they are fighting for and are confident of their own ability to win.'

The Vulture said nothing.

Paulus frowned almost as if he had expected the bandy-legged CO with his ugly mug to say something at that point. 'Your men for instance. They could do it, you know, Geier.

You were once in the Regular Army, they tell me, before you transferred,' Paulus sniffed disdainfully, 'to Herr Himmler's SS. You know what a victory of that kind would do for your promotion chances. They are crying out for me at the FHQ* to do something about Timoshenko. All the top people are watching this sector of the front. Probably the Führer will be himself . . . So,' he looked straight at Geier's ugly mug, 'it would mean a nice piece of tin to add to your throatache.' He indicated the Knight's Cross hanging around Geier's neck. 'And possibly, who knows, *your stars!*'

Von Dodenburg shot the Vulture a hard look. Both of them knew the men couldn't do it. They were exhausted. They had hardly enough men to crew the tanks. But the Vulture did not seem to notice that look. His eyes showed interest. 'I am very weak, sir,' he ventured.

'I know . . . I know . . .' Paulus said hastily. 'I only wish that I could send you a whole brand-new armoured battalion to back you up, give you more punch.'

Von Dodenburg groaned inwardly. The Vulture was buying it. Already the little wheels and cogs inside his devious brain were beginning to whirl and spin.

'But my strength, sir,' the Vulture tried again.

'I have rounded up a battalion of infantry for you,' Paulus said. 'It is not the best I must admit. In fact, it ran away last week.'

'A *German* battalion, sir?'

'Well, not exactly German, Geier,' Paulus answered. 'Italian to be specific. But they were not used to the conditions out here. Now they've found their feet. Their *Commando Supremo* had most of the battalion's officers shot last week. That's made them very much steadier.' Even the Vulture grinned and Paulus allowed himself a small cynical smile. 'They are the cannon-fodder you need to make the initial breakthrough, Geier,' he suggested. 'Stiffen them with a handful of your panzer grenadiers – fine-looking chaps, I

*The Führer's Headquarters

must say; let them take the casualties and wear the Russians down and let your tanks do the rest. It is a thought, isn't it, Geier.'

'It is indeed, sir.'

Von Dodenburg stared at them aghast. What cold-blooded calculation! They were prepared to sacrifice Wotan's young men, patriotic young believers in the Third Reich, not from any sense of patriotism or the cause, but for their own advantage – promotion, fame, glory; so that one day they would duly appear in the history books of the Second World War as the conqueror of this or that. For the first time in all the years he had been serving under the Vulture, Captain von Dodenburg realised his CO was not only a self-centred, cynical pervert, but also an absolutely ruthless egomaniac. Nothing was sacred to him. The Vulture wanted to be a general and he would not hesitate to sacrifice anyone or anything to that overruling passion. The first seeds of von Dodenburg's hatred for his CO had been sown.

'So there you have it, Geier. I will not prescribe your tactics, my dear fellow, naturally,' Paulus was saying. 'But let the Italians bear the brunt of the attack, while you pick up the . . . *laurels*. After all, there are enough of those spaghetti-eaters of Mussolini's as it is. Now, Colonel Geier, I must be on my way. The Italians arrive this evening. I expect you to attack at dawn.' Geier and von Dodenburg sprang to attention.

Casually Paulus touched his elegantly manicured hand to his cap. '*Hals und Beinbruch, meine Herren**,' he wished them and walked over to the waiting Mercedes.

'They've bought it, Heinz,' he whispered to his waiting aide as he entered. 'They always do, the gentlemen of the SS. They simply can't wait to die . . .'

Gloomily watching the proceedings, Schulze finished with his shirt and grunted. 'Do you think they'll give us a ration o' sauce before they send us in, Matzi?'

His comrade began tugging on his dice-beakers, as if he

---

*Roughly, 'happy landings'

were already preparing for what was to come. 'They allus do when they want yer to die a hero's death for folk, fatherland and Führer. Come on over to the goulash-cannon. Let's fill our guts with fart-food' – he meant pea-soup – 'before them thieving sods of kitchen bulls flog it all to the Popovs for cunt.'

Signor Coronel Brandt was big, blond, bold and worried; completely out of place among his swarthy little soldiers. 'South Tyrol, you know,' he had introduced himself in perfect Austrian German, bowing from the waist as he had saluted. 'Fought for the old Kaiser. Found myself a Macaroni four years later. Thought your Hitler would have taken us home into the Reich in '38. No such luck.' He had forced a bright-toothed grin. 'Ended up with this lot. Sicilian peasant boys, most of them not able to read or write. No wonder they ran away last week.'

Von Dodenburg had taken to the big officer straight away, but he saw his problem. His undersized teenage soldiers were plainly afraid of what was soon going to happen, and their NCOs went about carrying sub-machine guns threateningly over their shoulders, for obvious reasons. 'Regulars, you know, the noncoms . . . Romans for the most part . . . hate the guts of the Sicilians,' Brandt had explained. 'Shoot 'em out of hand at the first possible opportunity. What am I going to do with them, Herr von Dodenburg? A bunch of wops who play with themselves at night and think they're great lovers, Who've all got a powerful cousin in America, maybe Al Capone. He'll make them rich and powerful whenever Mussolini lets them emigrate. Wops who are condemned from the day they are born to go and work somewhere, in other countries than their own, perhaps seeing their mamas and papas once every five years or so. Herr von Dodenburg, they are *not* soldiers! They are uprooted frightened peasant boys who were born to lose!'

Von Dodenburg liked the big South Tyrolean; he loved his men. For him it would be a personal tragedy to have to throw their young lives away. He was no Vulture. All the same, *Signor Coronel* Brandt was going to have to do just that on the morrow. '*Herr Oberst*, I shall put it to you perfectly frankly. You and your men are to be our screen. I have been given the – er – honour of supporting you with our panzer grenadiers. You will cross the stream which held the Rumanians up. Then you will advance and take the foremost bunkers so that the tanks can start their attack. You will then –'

Colonel Brandt waved for him to stop. '*Will!*' he snapped. 'Excellent. I always like that firm military "will". Always sounds as if nothing, absolutely nothing, can go wrong.'

Von Dodenburg shared his smile.

Brandt's face grew serious again. 'We are going to be used as cannon-fodder, aren't we? Cover for your precious tanks.'

'I shall be supporting you myself, sir, with a small group of panzer grenadiers,' Von Dodenburg began, but then he knew he couldn't lie to this man. He nodded. 'Yessir, something like that.'

Brandt considered for a moment. Across on the other side of the camp one of his scared little soldiers began to sing sadly, gazing wistfully at the ascending moon. He nodded his head gravely. 'So be it. Well then, we *will* die a soldier's death. This time we won't run away.' Suddenly he thrust out his hand and as von Dodenburg took it he saw there were tears in the big soldier's eyes. 'You have my word on it . . .'

The long night passed slowly. Officially reveille was at two. Then they would move forward to the positions held by the Rumanians and cross the stream. At dawn the tanks would come in. That was officially. But the Italians were restless. They couldn't sleep. They whispered to one another in tense, anxious gasps. Here and there one of them sobbed like a broken-hearted child, calling for his 'mama'. And their NCOs, armed with their machine-pistols, patrolled their lines all the time, as if they half-expected the soldiers might well desert *en masse*.

It was little better in the Wotan lines. Although they were all veterans now, greenbeaks and old hares alike, the prospect of what lay ahead of them on the morrow drove all thoughts of sleep from their heads. Some lay in their blankets, hands beneath their heads, staring at the star-studded silver infinity of the night sky, as if they could hardly believe that under that same sky men and women lived in peace, were sound asleep now in clean, tidy beds, confident in the knowledge that they would live to sleep in those same beds another night. Some smoked fitfully, rising every now and again to urinate, a sure sign of nerves. A few, the real old hares such as Schulze and Matz, washed, changed their ragged, filthy underwear (in case they were hit; they were taking no chances of dirty linen being forced into the wounds to give them gangrene) and cleaned and oiled their weapons with thorough precision. They knew that on the morrow their very lives might depend upon those weapons functioning absolutely perfectly.

They chatted in the hushed, desultory fashion of men who worked late at night, with long, lazy pauses, hands cupped over the glowing red ends of their cigarettes, yawning now and again, farting occasionally, as if to show their contempt for fear. For they too were afraid. 'Sooner or later yer poor old frigging stubble-hopper goes hop and buys the farm,'* Schulze pronounced solemnly, taking the spring out of the machine-pistol he would soon be using and oiling it with almost loving care. 'There's no two sodding ways about it. We all bite into the shitting grass in the end.'

Matz took a long draw at his cigarette, as if he could not cram enough of the nerve-satisfying smoke into his lungs. 'But we've had good times too, Schulze,' he objected.

Schulze looked up from his spring, face hollowed out to a death's-head in the silver light of that expanse of cold, merciless stars. *'Good times*, Matzi!' he snorted with sudden anger. 'You must have air in yer frigging tooth! What kind of good times does yer common or garden shitting stubble-

*i.e. gets killed

hopper get? A bellyful of suds now and again, a couple of litres of giddi-up goulash* – if he's lucky with a piece of salami in it – and a quick feel of a pair of whore's tits! You call that a good time, you arse with frigging ears!'

'What do you want then, you big rogue,' a familiar voice cut in, 'egg in your shitting beer?'

The two of them struggled to get up, but von Dodenburg waved for them to remain seated.

Schulze grinned. 'Forget the egg – that's for nursing mothers. I'll settle for the suds.'

'I'll buy you a barrel personally when we've finished with this little lot, Schulze.'

'Ay, if it doesn't finish us first,' Schulze objected, grin vanishing as quickly as it had come. 'The Macaronis ain't got a chance. They'll either get their Eyetie turnips blown off by the Popovs or pick up their hindlegs and hoof it for all they're worth.'

'But *we* won't, Schulze,' Von Dodenburg said quietly.

'No, *we* won't!' Suddenly Schulze's voice was filled with bitterness. 'We'll stand and get our stupid turnips blown off or if we're cunning shits like Schulze or Matz or a couple of others I could mention, we might just get away with it. Perhaps just have a leg blown off, something harmless like that. So that we can wear our tin back home when we rattle our tin cups and cry, "Spare a mark for a disabled war hero!" All so the Vulture wins his shitting general's stars.'

'You're a cynic, Schulze,' von Dodenburg said, telling himself he should reprimand Schulze for talking like that but knowing, too, that he was right.

'Begging your pardon, sir,' Schulze said stubbornly. 'Not a cynic, but a realist. Look at all them lads. A year or so ago they were pressing the school-bank with their virginal, skinny arses. All full of shitting Goethe, whoever he is, and National Socialist spirit. Now they're plain killers, with not a spark of feeling left in them. They'd kill their own grandmas if they

*i.e. made of horsemeat

were ordered to.' He spat contemptuously. 'What good are they to society, even if they do frigging survive tomorrow, which they won't?'

Von Dodenburg remembered the Vulture's own cynical words on the same subject and felt a wave of anger well up within him. Those boys were the élite of the Third Reich, volunteers all, embued with the noble spirit of the New Order, which had shaken the old corrupt Europe to its foundations. 'We're the SS, Sergeant Schulze,' he said with anger and pride, 'the best Germany can produce, don't you know that?'

'With all due respect, sir, ' Schulze answered, noting the change in von Dodenburg's voice, 'I don't! They deserve to go hop tomorrow. The sooner they're planted and start looking at the taties from underneath, the better. We're killers . . .' Schulze broke off suddenly, as if he could continue no longer. 'Fuck it!' he mumbled and bent down over his spring once more.

Wordlessly von Dodenburg moved off into the silver-glowing night. So they waited while to their front the red signal flares hushed repeatedly into the night sky. It wouldn't be long now . . .

CHAPTER 5

A twig snapped.

Von Dodenburg spun round in the darkness angrily. 'I'll have the eggs off the next man who makes a damned noise – *with a blunt razorblade!*' he whispered threateningly.

"Fraid it was one of my people,' Colonel Brandt hissed back, as they crouched on the muddy bank of the little stream. 'They're a clumsy bunch.' He hissed an urgent order in Italian and his little soldiers bent their heads as if ashamed.

Von Dodenburg moved closer to the big Colonel. 'Tell them to wipe some of the mud on their hair. The Popovs have a terrific sense of smell. They can smell our people two or three hundred metres away.'

'It's that damned pomade they all use on their hair,' Brandt explained. 'But I'll tell them.'

Schulze, his good mood back now, sniggered, 'Oh, I wish I hadn't shaved and powdered my armpits now. All the Popovs will be after me!'

'Snout, hold yer snout!' the Butcher grunted, angry and scared that he had been selected for the little attack force.

'Frig you,' Schulze snapped back without rancour.

'All right,' von Dodenburg said, unslinging his machine-pistol, 'we go in first and take out the first trenches. You put in the main attack up the hill thereafter. All clear, Colonel?'

'All clear. And good luck, von Dodenburg.'

'Thank you, sir.' Von Dodenburg hesitated no longer. '*Mir nach!*' he commanded and waded swiftly into the water, holding his Schmeisser aloft, as it started to swirl up and up till it reached his waist. The others followed hurriedly. Once the Russians heard the noise they made there'd be trouble, and no one wanted to be caught in mid-stream.

Within minutes they were crouched on the other side, weapons at the ready, tense and eager, sniffing the air. For veterans as they were, they could smell a Russian from way off, too. They had long become aware of that typical Russian smell: a composite of black *marhokka* tobacco, sour black bread, boiled cabbage and human sweat.

'Over there, sir,' Matz hissed. 'At two o'clock. That's where they are.'

'Thanks, Matz. Yes, now I can see the parapets. All right, as little sound as possible. Use your weapons only in the last resort. Stick to knives and clubs. We've got to give Colonel Brandt's Italians the chance of surprise. Follow me.'

'Shitting spaghetti-eaters,' the Butcher sneered to cover his own fear. 'Couldn't frigging well fight their way out of a wet paper bag!'

Schulze sniffed, but said nothing. He concentrated on the task ahead.

Now they crept forward to where the first Russian line was, making little sound for such big men, their hearts thumping, their breath coming in tense little gasps. Von Dodenburg pointed to left and right. Wordlessly they followed his command and split into two groups, the Butcher conveniently positioning himself at the rear of the other group, away from von Dodenburg.

Von Dodenburg froze. Directly in front of him a face, a pale blur in the silver darkness, was staring at him. Below it was the earth-coloured smock of the Red army. For one long moment the German and the Russian stared at each other, transfixed. Slowly the Russian began to open his mouth.

Von Dodenburg did not give him the chance to sound the alarm. He sprang forward. With one hand he slapped the Russian against the side of his hole, with the other he drove home his combat knife. There was a terrible sucking noise. The Russian's spine arched like a taut bow. Von Dodenburg thrust home his knife again, feeling the hot blood flush his knuckles. The Russian gave a kind of sad gasp. Suddenly he slumped down – dead.

Now, like the cruel killers they were, the veterans spread out, slaughtering the surprised Russians silently, mercilessly.

Schulze silenced two with great blows from those cruel

brass knuckles of his, hearing them thwack audibly into the Russians' faces, splintering bone and tooth, splattering his hand right up to the wrist with gobs of bright crimson blood.

Matz worked differently. Springing on the Russians from behind, he ran his razor-sharp bayonet across their necks, slicing through the jugular as neatly as any butcher might have done, thrusting the two fingers of his other hand up his victim's nostrils to drown any cry he might attempt to make.

Within five minutes it was all over. They had taken the Russian first line without a single casualty, save for the Butcher who had apparently been hurt in the foot and was now slumped in one of the captured foxholes, moaning softly to himself. No one took any notice of him, however. 'Couldn't have happened to a nicer shit,' Schulze commented unfeelingly, wiping the blood of his 'Hamburg Equalizer' on the smock of a Russian he had just poleaxed. 'Perhaps the bone-menders'll have to saw his flipper off and we'll be rid of him for good.'

But that wasn't to be – just yet.

Now Brandt's little Italians were swarming forward, all helmet and overlong bayonet, quaking with fear. As they swept through the line of gasping men who had just taken the Russian position, the Wotan troopers could feel it; they *smelled* of fear! Von Dodenburg shook his head. Colonel Brandt was going to have his hands full. But he had other things to concern him now. 'All right, you heroes, don't just stand there thinking of all the medals you've just won. Let's get these Popov positions in order. You never know if we won't need their cover soon.' With that he bent and began to heave a dead Russian out of the nearest hole.

Suddenly the Butcher made a surprising recovery. As the thought shot through his mind that the Russians might well counter-attack, with startling suddenness he rose to his feet and began to dig furiously into the side of the foxhole.

Schulze laughed. 'Good for you, Sar'nt-Major,' he called. 'Never the one to moan, even when you've been hit.'

'Fuck off!' was Sergeant-Major Metzger's sole comment . . .

The bunker line above them erupted five minutes later. In an instant red signal flares were hissing into the sky on all sides and wild scarlet flame stabbed the darkness as the Italians charged. 'There the poor shits go!' Matz yelled as the black shapes of the little infantrymen were silhouetted against the sudden bursts of Russian fire.

'Poor sods,' Schulze agreed, pausing in his digging. 'They're for the chop, mark my words.' He shook his head, as if he had already dismissed them from his mind, and commenced digging once more.

Now the Wotan men could hear the screams, the yells for help, the cries of '*mama . . . mama*' as the Italians started going down everywhere in that devastating hail of enemy fire.

Von Dodenburg frowned and bit his lip grimly. It was still nearly two hours to dawn, but could the Italians seize the line before the arrival of the Vulture and the tanks? Somehow he doubted it. Then it would be up to him and his handful of veterans. Suddenly he clenched his fists with inner tension. Let the Italians take the bunker line, he prayed, let them take it!

Colonel Brandt wiped the blood from his face. Fifty metres away a Russian popped up and was about to lob a grenade. Brandt fired. The Russian reeled back and the grenade exploded harmlessly in front of his hole. '*Evivva Italia!*' Brandt cried, carried away by that old crazy illogic of battle. 'Come on, boys, let's have you!' He stared around at the men crouching in that shell-shattered lunar landscape. Their eyes, reflected in the lurid, garish light of the Russian flares, were black and liquid with fear and pain. He did not hesitate. He reached down and, grabbing the nearest soldier by the scruff of the neck, thrust him into the open.

A burst of MG fire hissed the length of the churned-up earth in front of them harmlessly. Brandt laughed out loud as if he were drunk. 'Did you see boys,' he cried. 'The Reds couldn't hit a barn-door, even if they wore specs! Follow the Colonel – he's got a hole in his arse!'

The old tricks worked. Suddenly new courage swept

through their skinny, undersized bodies. Soldiers were rising everywhere to follow the Colonel and the lone soldier, crying in their native dialect, struggling up the slope, springing over their own dead, zig-zagging around the shell-holes.

Once again the Russian bunkers spat fire. Men went down screaming everywhere. Huge gaps were ripped in the Italians' ranks. Still they kept on. Brandt felt a blow like a red-hot poker on his right shoulder. He dropped his revolver, the blood jetting from the second wound he had received. For a moment he thought he would fall. Somehow he kept going. If he stopped, he knew the steam would go out of this new attack. 'Come on, boys,' he yelled. 'Show them the Mafia is coming!'

His men laughed, dying with that laugh still spread on their dark pinched faces.

The first Russians started to come out of their holes, hands raised in surrender. The Italians didn't spare them. The bayonets flashed in the garish red light. Russians went down on all sides. Now the little Sicilians were dropping into the Russian trenches, bayonets flecked with blood. Brandt was hit again. He dropped to one knee, gasping with shock. One of his sergeants bent and picked him up by the arm. He forced a smile. They must not stop now.

Russian grenadiers came running down from above, throwing grenades to left and right. The Sicilians stood their ground. They felled the Russians with a concentrated volley and yelled with triumph. They were going to pull it off . . . *they were going to pull it off*, Brandt told himself, steadying himself against the wall of the trench, feeling very weak now.

The grenadiers had been replaced by other Russian infantry. For a long moment he could not make them out. Everything seemed to be hazy in front of his eyes now. Why were the Russians attacking in such heavy packs? You never sent in attacking infantry weighed down like that. Suddenly he gasped. The last time he had seen soldiers like that, burdened with round packs, carrying what looked like rubber tubes in their hands, they had been Italians:

Italians counter-attacking the Austrian Army on the Piave.

'*Flame throwers!*' someone screamed in absolute fear, as the
first of the Russians pressed the trigger of his terrible weapon
and a long stream of ugly purple flame hissed towards the
Italian positions, slapping the newly-captured bunkers with a
fiery rod. Abruptly the air was full of the stink of burned oil –
and scorched flesh.

'Knock them out, you riflemen . . . Knock them out!'
Brandt cried desperately as one of his men went reeling back,
suddenly a startling black, the flames leaping ever higher up
his body until his face, transformed into a horrid, charred
skull, disappeared.

'Don't run . . . hit them!' He fired wildly at the leading
Russian. The man went down on his knees and in his death
throes, finger glued to his trigger, he hosed his own comrades
with that terrible, all-consuming flame. Half a dozen of them
ran, shrieking hysterically, the greedy flames hushing up
their bodies, their steps getting weaker by the moment until
finally, they too fell and surrendered to that awesome fire.

But the damage had been done. Everywhere the survivors
of the Italian charge were crouching low in their trenches and
among the shattered pillboxes, throwing down their weapons
to dig deeper with frantic haste.

Colonel Brandt slumped and suddenly he found his legs
going from beneath him like those of a newborn foal. He sat
down abruptly, all strength and determination draining from
his big body as if someone had just opened a tap. 'In a
minute,' he said weakly, as his officers scrambled forward to
assist him. 'I'll be all right in a minute . . . Just give me time to
catch my breath . . .'

About the same time that the steam went out of the Italian
attack, a terribly scared Butcher, still digging for all he was
worth, realised that he was not alone in the foxhole. There
was no mistaking it. In the far corner, barely glimpsed in the
lurid light that came from the embattled pillbox line, he

could see a strange little shape crouched there – *and the shape was armed!*

He blinked his eyes several times, heart thumping madly, his limbs abruptly turned to water. Yes, there was no mistaking it. All the time he had been digging, he had not been alone. But was the shape dead? And what was the matter with it? Where the face should have been there was a strange distorted kind of mask, an odd mixture of beige, green and dark brown hues.

His hand trembling visibly, he reached out, breath coming in short, hectic gasps as if he had just run a race, and touched it. *It was still alive!*

The Butcher nearly fainted. The thing was Russian, he knew, and it was alive, only a metre away from where he now knelt, his big brutal body shaking as if he had a fever. 'What . . .' he tried to croak. 'What –'

Suddenly the frightening thing flung itself upon him. He reeled back, taken by surprise. But instinctively he reacted. His big paws reached out for the thing's throat, missed, and found themselves grabbing soft, female flesh. *The thing was a woman!* And then he realised with whom he was dealing; it all came to him in a flash. She was one of those celebrated Russian woman snipers, who stayed behind, allowing themselves to be overrun by the Germans so that they could commence their bloody work to the unsuspecting Germans' rear. 'Why, you Popov bitch!' he cried, all his strength returning to him in a great surge as he realised that he was dealing with a mere woman; and Sergeant-Major Metzger had never been afraid of women, well, up to quite recently at least. *'Find 'em, feel 'em, frig 'em and forget 'em!'* That had always been his proud boast to his cronies in the sergeants' mess in the old days.

But he was not going to have it all his own way. The woman cursed in Russian, wriggled suddenly and freed herself from his grasp, the cloth of her camouflaged tunic ripping as she did so to reveal two startlingly white breasts.

Sergeant-Major Metzger gulped. Next moment his gulp of

amazement had changed to a gasp of pain, as she nearly
successfully kneed him. He swung back his big paw. With all
his strength he slapped her hard across the face. She gave a
little sigh and abruptly her struggles ended and he was on top
of her, feeling her soft female flesh and that old familiar,
wonderful stirring in his loins as he thrust them into the
delightful cushion of her pelvis. Moments later he was ripping
at her clothes, tearing them apart savagely, eyes gleaming
greedily, as that faint stirring became a hard certainty. He
forced her legs open and then he was fumbling crazily at his
flies with fingers that trembled with excitement. One minute
later it was happening and the Butcher forgot the war, the
danger, his own fear, in the ecstasy of that absolute sheer
delight. *It was working again!*

The huge shell tore the silence apart terrifyingly. With a
hellish crash it slammed to the torn-up earth only a hundred
metres away from Brandt's bunker. Flame spurted high. Earth
erupted in a mad fountain. The bunker trembled. One of
Brandt's officers cried in agony. He fell the next instant, the
back of his head a bloody mess. 'They're bringing down fire
on their own line!' Brandt cried, fighting to regain his
strength. 'That means they're going to counter-attack . . . Be
prepared, men, they're coming –'
    Another shell plunged to the ground and drowned the rest
of his words. The ground shimmied and shivered. The very
air was snatched from their lungs. Pebbles and earth rained
down on their bent, helmeted heads.
    Now the whole weight of the Russian bombardment
descended upon the hilltop line. The huge shells made no
distinction between Russian and Italian. They fell on both
their positions, separated from one another by a mere two
hundred metres. The pre-dawn became a red-roaring,
screaming nightmare. Shrapnel, fist-sized, silver and glowing,
flew everywhere. Piteously screaming, the little Sicilians
cowering in the bottoms of their pits, nether limbs soaked in

their own waste, fingering their rosaries desperately, were scythed down. Here and there they couldn't stand it. They broke from cover, throwing away their weapons, only to be ripped apart before they had gone a couple of metres. A man went mad. He stumbled out into no man's land, screaming at the top of his voice, waving his fist, and nearly reached the nearest Russian bunker before he was ripped down by a cruel burst of tracer . . .

On and on it went, this terrible barrage. For those few who survived, it could have lasted, or so it seemed, a matter of years. In fact, it was barely twenty minutes before it stopped, leaving behind a loud-echoing, brooding silence.

'Stand to! Tell the men to stand to,' Colonel Brandt said weakly to his officers, who crouched round him in the dugout, pale-faced and shaken. 'They'll be coming soon . . . mark my words!'

Somehow Colonel Brandt's steadiness had its effect, though they could see he was dying; for now his face was ashen and pinched-nosed, sure signs of approaching death. They shrilled their whistles. NCOs bellowed orders. Those who had survived that tremendous bombardment dragged themselves out of the steaming earth and stared in amazement at this transformed world, now revealed in all its ugliness in the first dirty white light of the new dawn.

'Stand to . . . stand to . . !' the cry went from foxhole to foxhole.

Nervously, electric with tension, the Sicilians took up their positions – but not for long.

Soviet flares started to sail into the air to their front; red, green, white and then – violet. Brandt knew what that violet flare signified and his heart sank. The Soviets were going to attack with tank support. Now more than ever he needed the Germans with those massive Tigers of theirs.

The Vulture dropped from the deck of the dripping Tiger, the first to cross the stream, seemingly not noticing the lone

Soviet machine-gun which had opened up at it like an angry woodpecker.

Von Dodenburg straightened to attention.

The Vulture waved his cane angrily. 'No time for playing soldier, von Dodenburg,' he snapped. 'So the macaronis haven't taken it, eh?'

'Doesn't look like it, sir,' von Dodenburg agreed staring at that shattered, jagged hilltop, outlined in the new dawn. 'At least not all of it.'

The Vulture shook his head. 'No use wasting any more time. Mount up your chaps, von Dodenburg. We've got to take our chance that all the Russian anti-tank guns have been knocked out. But we can't afford to hang about. We get through this morning or we don't get through at all. Clear?'

'Clear, sir,' von Dodenburg answered reluctantly. The Tigers were going to attack positions which were ideally suited to defence against slow-moving tanks. But there was nothing *he* could do about it. 'We'll lose the Regiment, sir,' he said, making one final try. 'If there are anti-tank guns still working up there, sir, they'll pick us off one by one.'

The Vulture waved his cane impatiently. 'What do I care? Give me one Tiger, one lone Tiger, on the other side of that damned hill and we've won. We've broken through the line. Now let us not stand here gossiping like fishwives. Let's be off.'

'*Zu Befehl, Obersturmbannführer!*' von Dodenburg snapped, using the old military formula ironically. But irony was wasted on the Vulture this dawn. He was too eager for victory – *and those general's stars!*

Now the veterans were clambering out of their holes to meet the advancing tanks, rising like ghosts from their graves. Only the Butcher hesitated. He crouched there while the girl stared at him, her mask removed now to reveal a broad, Slavic peasant face beneath corn-yellow cropped hair. 'You liked it, didn't you, wench?' he said proudly, buttoning up his flies.

She stared at him blankly. '*Horoscho?*' he attempted,

making an obscene gesture with his fingers. '*Horoscho* – ficki-ficki with *nmetski?*' He laughed. 'German sausage good for Ivan, *da . . . da?*'

Slowly, very slowly she nodded her cropped head, but her eyes revealed nothing. She had been a virgin, but that hadn't mattered. As he had always guffawed to his cronies in the sergeants' mess, 'The only difference between a wench who's had a length of salami before and a virgin is that it *hurts* with a virgin. Ha ha!'

Up front the Vulture was shouting his head off and he wondered if he shouldn't just duck out now, while he was safe. There was trouble ahead, he knew that.

He finished buttoning up his flies and bent to pick up his helmet. She still hadn't moved, but squatted there, with her legs still spread, the bright red blood trickling down her inner thigh. He grinned. When Metzger screwed them, they stayed screwed. They'd never like another man after him.

He chuckled happily to himself in spite of the imminent prospect of action as more and more of the battle-scarred Tigers splashed across the stream like great metal ducks. There weren't many men with a stick of salami that could match Sergeant-Major Metzger's. 'If you stay there, wench,' he cried, bent down now, 'I'll come back and give you another taste of the –'

His proud boast ended in a sudden groan as the rock crashed down on the back of his shaven skull. He staggered forward, face almost touching the ground, fighting off unconsciousness, bright red stars exploding in front of his eyes. '*Boshe moi!*' the girl he had raped cried, 'Die, pig . . . *DIE!*' She hit him again with all her strength and the Butcher went out like a light. For one instant she looked down at him, his skull mashed and bloody, then she spat on him and was gone, leaving him for dead. But the Butcher was not fated to die. Indeed that unknown girl sniper might well have saved the big NCO's life that morning. *For now Wotan's ride of death had commenced . . .*

CHAPTER 6

'GIOVINEZZA!' The officers chanted the popular fascist song as that hoarse Russian 'urrah . . . urrah' came ever closer and the massed Russian storm battalions came stamping out of the fog of war. But the rank and file were not inspired. They crouched in their holes, their dark Latin faces greased with sweat, eyes wild and liquid with fear. The Russians were coming!

Brandt took a swig of the *grappa* he carried in his water-bottle and felt the fiery liquid sock into his stomach. He gasped and his head grew a little clearer. He was bleeding badly now – his shirt was full of clammy, warm blood – but he was still alive and he was thinking.

The Reds had made the mistake of lifting their barrage too early. Now that brown mass advancing on them, their bayonets gleaming in the first rays of the sun like a wall of lances, would be an easy target. It was the tanks which worried him. He shook his head and his eyes came into focus with difficulty. He searched that ruined lunar landscape, pitted with shell-holes, the dead, Russian and Italian, hanging on the rusting barbed wire like bundles of rags. There wasn't a tank in sight. Had he been mistaken about that signal?

'*Signore Coronel!*' It was Pietro, his adjutant, handsome and dashing, a typical flamboyant Roman.

'Yes?'

'Have I your permission to command open fire, sir?' he asked very formally.

Brandt chuckled to himself and winced with pain the next moment. How comic opera this army of foreigners, for which he would soon die, was! 'Yes,' he gasped, 'you have my permission, Pietro.'

The Roman wasted no time. He jumped onto the parapet of the hole he shared with the Colonel and stood there, playing the hero, foolishly erect and in full view of the advancing Russians. 'Soldiers,' he declared boldly. 'Sons of the wolf! Prepare to open fire. *FI –*'

The command ended in a scream of absolute agony as a machine-gun from one of the Russian-held pillboxes opened up. Suddenly his face looked as if someone had just thrown a handful of strawberry jam at it, as he fell dead to the ground in the same instant that the whole Italian line erupted in a ragged volley.

The whole front rank of the Russians went down. Even the Sicilians could not miss those packed ranks. Abruptly the Russians were galvanised into electric activity, swinging round crazily, throwing down their weapons, crumpling in vicious fury, falling . . . falling . . . falling everywhere.

'Bravo . . . bravo, boys!' Brandt called, raising himself so that his men could see him and know he was still alive. 'Do it again . . . once more for me, boys!' His words ended in a fit of coughing.

Suddenly the Sicilians grew bold. They set to work with a will, pouring fire into the advancing ranks of the Russians. They went down in dreadful numbers now. That bold '*urrah*' ceased. Now the survivors were beginning to hesitate. Here and there officers clambered over the writhing bodies of the dying, waving their swords and urging the men to come on. The flag-bearer, carrying that blood-red standard of Soviet Russia, heaved it back and forth encouragingly until he too went down, his chest smashed in by a vicious burst of fire.

The survivors started to back off, in spite of the threats, pleas and curses of their officers, firing as they moved down the slope once more, but still backing off.

Brandt laughed. His Sicilians had done it. They had beaten the Russians! Now was the time for him to counter-attack. 'Fix bayonets, my brave boys!' he commanded and to his surprise, he could hear the click of steel upon steel everywhere. They were actually carrying out his order. Their little victory had put new heart into them.

Somehow or other he pulled himself to his feet in the hole,

swaying violently with weakness but knowing he had to lead from the front; he had to. 'Prepare to –'

The words died on his lips. Three squat T-34s had emerged from the smoke to the left, crunching over the bodies of their own dead, their tracks flushing a sudden red. Someone in the Italian line reacted instantly. Anti-tank bullets sprayed towards the three tanks. They bounced off uselessly like glowing ping-pong balls. Brandt sank down again helplessly, letting it happen.

It did. The battalion broke. Suddenly they were throwing away their weapons in their haste to escape the monsters and streaming down the slope, screaming and shrieking with fear, jostling and clawing each other in their unreasoning terror.

Brandt waited. He knew what would come. But he didn't care any more. His Sicilians had broken. They would never be reformed. It was useless.

Now the monster was above him as he slumped there in the pit alone and abandoned. The din was tremendous. His ears were deafened by the terrific roar, his nostrils full of the cloying stink of diesel oil. Already he could feel the hot oil drip onto his upturned face from the engine, as the driver started to turn round and round, revving the engine, flooding his hole with that deadly gas. He felt the air being sucked cruelly from his lungs. He started to gasp. He was choking. More and more began to trickle down. The pit was crumbling. He let it happen . . .

'*Panzer vorne!*' The Vulture rapped on the turret of the Tiger he was riding on together with von Dodenburg, Schulze and Matz. '*Los, Mensch . . . Feuer!*'

The gunner pulled his firing bar. Von Dodenburg opened his mouth automatically to prevent his eardrums from being burst. The long cannon spat fire. At a tremendous rate the huge shell went hurtling – a dazzling white blur – towards the T-34 which had suddenly appeared out of the smoke.

The T-34 reared up like a wild horse being put to the

saddle for the first time. Next moment it crashed down, its cannon falling limply to one side, smoke pouring from it. No one got out.

Now T-34s were appearing from all sides. Hanging on for dear life, von Dodenburg gasped. He had never seen so many Russian tanks before. The enemy was obviously determined to fight for this damned nameless hilltop to the bitter end; he knew what was at stake.

'Christ on a crutch!' Matz gasped. 'Look at the Popov pricks! They're every-frigging-where!'

'Yer get yer share of 'em,' Schulze snarled, as tracer zipped towards them in a lethal morse. 'Get yer frigging stupid turnip . . . *down!*' He shoved Matz down on the heaving deck, just as a salvo of slugs ripped the length of the Tiger like a boy running an iron bar along some railings. The Vulture yelped and clapped his hand to his shoulder, his fingers suddenly flushed with blood. 'Dammit!' he cursed. 'Von Dodenburg, if anything happens to me, you're in charge.'

Von Dodenburg forced a grin, though he had never felt less like grinning. 'And who gets those famous general's stars, sir?' he asked.

'Oh shut up,' the Vulture snapped and sat down suddenly.

Now the drama commenced. Shells thudded back and forth in blazing white fury. T-34 after T-34 was hit. They came to sudden stops, blazing immediately for the most part, their crews fleeing for their lives only to be mown down mercilessly as they ran for cover.

But the Tigers were taking casualties too. At that range even their thick steel hide could be penetrated. And now the slope leading up to the top was marked here and there by a limping, dying Tiger, its side scarred and gnarled a bright new silver by the Russian shells which had finally brought about its death. The Vulture would brook no halting. The blood streaming down his wounded arm unheeded, he was in the middle of the fray, yelling orders, threatening, at times drawing his pistol when scared young commanders seemed reluctant to go on, urging his men ever onwards, knowing that once the momentum was lost they would never make that hilltop. In spite of the Vulture's complete disregard for the lives of his young men, von Dodenburg could not but admire his leadership. It was the Vultures of this world who won battles, he told himself, as the Tiger rocked again under the impact of yet another direct hit and his nostrils were assailed by the stink of burned paint and fused steel.

A group of Russian soldiers ran blindly towards the Vulture's Tiger, as if they were eager to surrender. At the very last moment, von Dodenburg noticed the bottles they held in their upraised hands. 'Molotov cocktails!' he cried urgently.

'Treacherous bastards!' Schulze yelled and swung up his Schmeisser and firing instantly.

The Russians were bowled over, the anti-tank devices falling from their suddenly nerveless hands. But Schulze was not letting them off so lightly. He took careful aim. The nearest bottle exploded in a searing burst of blue flame, throwing the burning liquid over those Russians feigning death, turning them into writhing, screaming torches. Schulze laughed crazily.

Now they were nearly there, but the punishment was telling. Another Tiger was hit. In an instant it was a bubbling cauldron of steel, its small arms ammunition exploding and zig-zagging crazily into the livid, burning sky like a New Year's Eve fireworks display. Suddenly with a muffled boom the whole ammunition locker exploded and what looked like a huge white smoke ring blown by a giant began to ascend slowly out of its turret. No one got out.

A low roar began which suddenly became a high-pitched, baleful scream and rose to a furious elemental howl, blotting out all other sound. The fiery missiles came screeching out of the sky, bursting everywhere, striking both Russian and German. 'Stalin organs!' the Vulture screamed, as to their left a pillbox disappeared, scattering dismembered bodies on all sides and drenching the side of the Tiger in the blood of the slaughtered. '*Tempo, driver . . . Tempo!*' In his rage and fear, he slapped the side of the turret furiously with his cane; and von Dodenburg knew why. If the feared Soviet rocket cannon zeroed in on them, they would be finished.

Below, the sweating driver put his foot down hard on the massive pedal. The Tiger gathered speed. Behind them more and more of the rockets came plunging out of the sky frighteningly. Another Tiger was hit and simply disintegrated, all sixty tons of it. When the smoke cleared, all that was left of it was a lone bogey wheel trundling down the slope.

An anti-tank gun opened up towards their left. A tremendous blow struck the Tiger next to the Vulture's. It reeled as if struck by a tornado. 'Get it . . . Get it, von Dodenburg!' the Vulture screamed.

As one, the three dropped from the moving Tiger. In the lead, von Dodenburg sprayed the metal shield of the Soviet 57mm, while Schulze and Matz, taking advantage of the diversion he was creating, doubled to the flank.

'*One!*' Schulze cried and pulled the china pin out of his stick grenade. '*TWO!*' Matz yelled, doing the same. '*THREE!*' they bellowed together and heaved their bombs.

The surprised Russian anti-tank crew slumped over their shattered breach, and next moment the three of them were running back to the waiting Tiger, lead stitching the ground at their flying feet.

Now there seemed to be only three Tigers left, glimpsed briefly through the billowing clouds of smoke and the furious red bursts of flame. Whether there were any others surviving beyond the barrage put down by the Stalin organs, the Vulture neither knew nor cared. He still had three 'runners' and the way ahead was open. 'We've got them, von Dodenburg!' he yelled exuberantly, as the young officer swung himself aboard the deck, gasping like an ancient asthmatic. '*We've got them!*'

Next to the officer Schulze shook his head as if he could not believe his own ears. 'With three tanks, we've beaten a frigging Popov army! Oh, my aching back!'

'*Wenn die Nonnen stoehnen in den Klostern, dann wird's Ostern!*'*
Matz said philosophically, though at that moment his
meaning was not quite clear to his old running-mate.

But the Vulture, wounded as he was, did not heed their
attitudes or comments. 'It is dash that counts, comrades!' he
yelled above the *thump thump* of yet another salvo of rockets. 'A
hundred metres more – no, *fifty* – and they'll run. I know they
will. They'll take their heels under their arms and run from
here to Moscow!'

A T-34 loomed up in front of them, then another. But the
fight was going from the Russians. The Russian saw the lone
Tiger and swung round. In their panicked haste, both drivers
lost their heads. They slammed into each other with a
resounding boom. Schulze didn't wait for a second invitation.
'Vodka . . . frigging vodka!' he cried and sprang from the
Tiger, followed by Matz. Together they pelted towards the
stalled T-34s, followed by von Dodenburg's angry cries for
them to stop.

But carried away by the heady excitement of combat,
nothing could stop them now. A grenade through the driver's
slit of the first tank, a burst of machine-pistol fire into the
turret of the second one and in an instant a frantic bunch of
bleeding, pleading Russians were pouring out of the two
tanks, while the two NCOs searched them for vodka,
knocking the heads off the two bottles they found and
draining them, glass and all, while the Soviets stood quaking
and watched them.

On and on they went, Schulze and Matz singing crazily
now, eyes glazed and faces flushed with vodka. To their right,
one of the remaining three Tigers breasted the height far too
slowly. Von Dodenburg yelled a warning. The fool of a driver
was presenting his soft belly to any Soviet gunner, on a
damned silver tray. Tensely he waited for the inevitable as
next to him a completely drunk Schulze bellowed, '*I love my
wife . . . I love her dearly . . . I love the hole she pisses through . . .*'

---

*'When the nuns sigh in the cloisters, then it is Easter'

Nothing happened! The Tiger disappeared safely over the rise. Not a shot had been fired.

A moment later they had breasted the rise themselves to view the mass of men and machines fleeing wildly to the east below, streaming away in their panic, a broken, hysterical rabble. Suddenly von Dodenburg sat down, all energy spent, completely exhausted. They had done it . . . They had done it! The ride of death was over.

Leaning weakly against the big cannon, as the Tiger slowly rumbled to a stop, the Vulture, his face pale with loss of blood, cried with the last of his strength. 'My stars . . . *I won my shitting stars!'*

Envoi

'Fuck 'em all, fuck 'em all, the long and the short and the tall. You'll get no promotion this side of the ocean, so cheer up my lads, *fuck 'em all!*'
[*WWII British marching song.*]

THE GROUP of Storch observation planes hit the steppe one after another in bursts of dust and rolled to a stop directly in front of that handful of worn men standing rigidly to attention on the parched grass, the sweat streaming down their haggard faces.

Immediately, waiting orderlies flung open the doors and clicked to attention as the important visitors began to descend in their elegant, decorated tunics and highly polished boots. The Vulture, arm still in a sling, tensed. This was it. Behind him Schulze farted deliberately to show his contempt for the whole stupid business. For his part, von Dodenburg frowned. Nothing was left of the Regiment now. Had it all been just for this silly little ceremony? Indeed, at that moment, there seemed to be only one happy individual present in the middle of that burning steppe, and that was *Sonderführer* Pegleg Izzy. After all, it wasn't every day that a one-legged former knicker-elastic salesman received a medal for bravery from a well-known German gentleman!

The generals took their time, chatting and laughing among themselves, while the busy orderlies flicked the dust from their boots and tugged at the back of tunics which had ridden up in the long flight from Paulus's new headquarters in Stalingrad. A couple of of them even unscrewed silver flasks containing spirits and offered them to others. And all the while. Colonel-General Paulus, the victor at Stalingrad, towering above the rest, smiled vainly, pleased beyond measure with himself.

'Look at the pompous shit-heap,' Schulze whispered out of the corner of his mouth to Matz, 'yer'd think the frigging sun shone out of his arse!'

'Sixteen thousand men it takes to train a Major-general,' Marshal Joffre had once remarked cynically, von Dodenburg told himself, as he watched Paulus's posturing. 'How many does it take to make a fieldmarshal?' For that, he knew, was what Paulus was after. Like the Vulture, now so eager and expectant in spite of his weariness, the tall General was an obvious glory hunter.

Suddenly the generals formed up. The Reichsführer SS was ready to inspect his men. The Vulture tensed. Pegleg Izzy threw out his skinny chest proudly. Schulze farted again for good measure. And von Dodenburg just suppressed a cry of utter despair at the very last moment.

The Vulture waited until the spindly-legged, sallow-faced head of the SS with his weak, receding chin and schoolmaster's pince-nez had come to a stop, surrounded by the generals. Then he marched forward the regulation six paces and, clicking to attention in a cloud of dust, bellowed at the top of his voice, '*SS Sturmregiment Wotan – angetreten, Reichsführer!*'

Himmler's mouth dropped open and the arm he had been raising to salute the Vulture with the 'German greeting' stopped in mid-air. 'Did you . . . you say, this is . . . *your regiment, Obersturmbannführer?*' he quavered in absolute, total disbelief.

'*Jawohl, Reichsführer!*' the Vulture barked, noticing over Himmler's bent right shoulder that Paulus was watching the little scene, his vain face filled with boredom.

Himmler's dark eyes behind a suddenly clouded pince-nez filled with tears. 'My brave boys,' he whispered huskily to himself. 'My poor brave boys.' He took his pince-nez off and rubbed it clear, looking more of a provincial schoolmaster than ever. A few metres away one of his 'poor brave boys', namely Sergeant Schulze, whispered to Corporal Matz, 'Look at the four-eyed prick! He's gonna go into a migraine in half a mo.'

But that didn't happen. Instead Himmler conquered his emotions and clicked his fingers.

Promptly a blond giant in black uniform, who stood at least half a head taller than Schulze, strode forward, bearing a basket heaped with cheap, bright pieces of enamel.

The Vulture beamed. They were going to be decorated. Soon he'd ask about his 'stars'.

'Tin!' Matz sneered contemptuously, as Himmler started to go down the line of the survivors, shaking hands, pinning on medals, saying a few words to each soldier. 'I've got a frigging drawer full of the stuff already!'

'Ask him for the scrambled egg,'* Schulze suggested as Himmler paused a little uncertainly in front of *Sonderführer* Pegleg Izzy, 'you ain't got that one in yer collection yet. It'll be good for a couple of litres of suds when we've achieved final victory, *I don't think!*'

'*Sonderführer . . . Schmidt!*' The Vulture found a suitably Germanic name hurriedly, as Himmler stared at Pegleg Izzy's swarthy face and hooked nose a little uncertainly. 'Locally recruited. An excellent soldier and comrade.'

Pegleg's chest swelled even more.

'First or second, *Reichsführer?*' the black-clad giant holding the basket asked.

Himmler peered hard through his pince-nez. 'Schmidt, eh,' he mused and made his decision. 'Second class, please!'

A moment later Pegleg Izzy's pigeon chest was decorated with the Iron Cross, Second class and Himmler had passed on to decorate yet another hero.

'And now, Colonel Geier,' he said finally, 'it is your turn. Altmann, the laurel leaves for *Obersturmbannführer* Geier!' he commanded his adjutant.

Geier caught a whiff of Himmler's aftershave as the medal was hung around his neck and then Himmler was pressing his hand in his own two soft, rather clammy fists in the style of the Führer. It was now or never, he told himself. 'Reichsführer,' he ventured.

'Yes, Geier?' Himmler beamed at him through the pince-nez.

'I hear . . . ah . . . I was *sorry* to hear that *Standartenführer* Eicke had fallen in battle for . . . folk, fatherland and Führer,'

*Soldiers' slang for the 'German Cross in Gold', a high award he added hurriedly, knowing that sort of thing would please the skinny little ex-chicken farmer; he liked that sort of cheap patriotic gush.

Himmler's eyes flushed with tears once more. 'Yes, poor dear Papa* has departed from us in this terrible war. But why do you ask, Geier?'

'This, sir. His death on the battlefield – so bravely – means that the *Totenkopf*** Division needs a new commander . . . er . . . a general officer . . .'

Himmler nodded his agreement. 'Exactly, my dear Geier, exactly.' Now Himmler understood what the ugly colonel with his monocle and gross lecher's face was after. He smiled bleakly. 'But those general's stars will not go to you, Geier.'

The Vulture flushed. 'But why not, sir? I have commanded a full regiment long enough. This breakthrough is undoubtedly –'

Himmler held up his flabby paw for silence. 'The losses of the SS in Russia have been tremendous, Geier. The cream of German youth has fallen here, and that cream – the elite of the elite – must be replaced. Every SS man, whatever his rank, must play his role, work hard to make up for those losses.'

The Vulture listened in bewilderment, wondering what the fool was talking about. What had all this twaddle to do with his general's stars?

Finally Himmler told him. 'From last week onwards, Geier, I have ordered that there will be no further promotions in my SS.'

'No further promotions, *Reichsführer?*' the Vulture stuttered.

'Yes. For officers who are *single!* The future of the race is at stake. It is the duty of every SS man to produce at least three children.' He wagged his finger under the Vulture's great beak of a nose. 'Everyone, old or young, must do his bit. The nation needs fresh blood!'

*Nickname given to Eicke by his men
**The Fourth SS Division, 'The Death's Head', which had been commanded by Eicke

The Vulture swallowed hard. 'Do you mean, sir, that . . . that only officers who . . . are married,' he stuttered, 'will be promoted henceforth . . ?' He looked at Himmler's sallow face incredulously.

'Exactly, Geier. Marry and we can have another think about those General's stars.' Himmler's right arm shot out. '*Heil Hitler!*' he barked.

'*Heil Hitler!*' The Vulture echoed weakly, his voice seeming to come from kilometres away, his vision suddenly blurred, his legs as weak as those of a babe. '*Marry?*' he croaked as the brass began to head back to the plane. '*Marry! Not that!*'

Minutes later they had gone, bearing with them General Paulus, heading for his own particular date with destiny, leaving behind a shattered Vulture whose whole world had fallen apart, and a bunch of grinning veterans sprawled now in the cropped grass, tunics tugged open, enjoying this little respite before it all began yet again.

Captain von Dodenburg leaned against a tree in the shade, smoking moodily while watching them. But he saw not only their tough worn faces, but also those of the ghosts – the Pill, Dietz and the rest, hundreds, thousands of them: a host of them, pale, staring, dead, who would march with them for ever. Slowly he took a drag of his cigarette, numb with a sudden sense of loss. SS Assault Regiment Wotan had been decimated yet again. Abruptly Kuno von Dodenburg felt very old.

But Sergeant Schulze and his old comrade Corporal Matzi had no time for regret and sadness this day. They knew, 'old hares' that they were, that the sacrifice of all those brave boys who would never see the Homeland again meant that *they* had been saved for a few more months.

'Don't yer realise, ape-turd,' Schulze yelled suddenly, face flushed crimson with the *Kognak* that Himmler's adjutant had presented to the survivors, 'we're going home! Home to mother!' He took a huge gulp from his flatman and waved the gift cigar like a baton. 'By the Great Whore of Buxtehude where the dogs bark with their tails, Matzi, *we're going home!*'

Suddenly the big NCO's heady excitement infected the others. The drink helped too. '*We're going home, comrades!*' they cried, realising that they were at last. '*Imagine it, wading through female tits up to yer knees . . . Suds and sauce, as much as yer want, till it comes out of yer ears . . . Cunt by the cartload . . . Titty-rolls and trombone practice every day. . !*' From all sides the excited, drunken cries rose up as they sprawled there on that burning, nameless steppe, flushed with the heat, drink and excitement: '*SS ASSAULT REGIMENT WOTAN IS GOING H-O-M-E . . !*'